# THE MATTER OF THE
# RUNAWAY
# BULLION FLATCAR

## THE 800 POUNDS OF GOLD FOR A
## DOZEN STUDENTS CAPER

### STEVE LEVI
Master of the Impossible Crime

PUBLICATION
CONSULTANTS
WE BELIEVE IN THE POWER OF AUTHORS

PO Box 221974 Anchorage, Alaska 99522-1974
books@publicationconsultants.com—www.publicationconsultants.com

ISBN 978-1-63747-073-2
ebook ISBN 978-1-63747-074-9

Library of Congress Catalog Card Number: 2021953146

"A great detective is like a child; he doesn't know that some things are impossible."

. . . Heinz Noonan .

Just because something is obvious
does not make it true.

. . . Detective Heinz Noonan

# CHAPTER 1

Heinz Noonan, "the Bearded Holmes" of the Sandersonville Police Department, was up to his kneecaps in the great dismal swamp. This, however, was not the infamous Great Dismal Swamp which spanned one million acres of southeastern Virginia and northeastern North Carolina. It was, alas, one in which the Sandersonville Commissioner of Homeland Security had condemned him to wallow therein. This swamp was one of politics, and Noonan had been ordered to not only *attend* but **quarterback** a police-citizens interface. The Sandersonville Citizens Interface, SCI, which the Commissioner incorrectly pronounced as "ski" was a chance for community members to express their feelings – pro and con but mostly con – of the local police force.

It was the worst all possible assignments for a front-line crime fighter. Front-line crime fighters spend their time scouring the earth for the scum of the community, the very individuals SCI people want off the street, out of their community and in the hoosegow for lengthy sentences. These front-line crime fighters are seasoned street tumblers and ill-equipped to sit on park benches cheek-to-jowl with chamber of commerce types who were more concerned with drunks on the sidewalk than peripatetic opioid salesmen. If SCI had been just the camaraderie of an afternoon of eating burgers and shaking hands, it would have been tolerable.

Alas, such was not the case.

**Quarterbacking** an SCI meeting necessarily meant ongoing meetings dealing with well-meaning people who had no idea what a police department was supposed to do or actually did. Because of this civic ignorance, these citizens had no idea how well – or poorly – their local police were doing their jobs. Worse, these members of the community could not – or would not – distinguish one internal department from another or, for that matter, State Troopers from local police. So there would be citizens irate at a parking ticket from Avon complaining to the Sandersonville Police Department or a speeding ticket from the State Troopers.

Noonan was bracing himself for the upcoming moron-a-thon when the tool of Satan, the diabolic electronic gadget, the cursed gizmo from Hell itself, began vibrating in his cargo pants pocket. Cursing the man, woman, team, and company who had come up with the concept of a cell phone, iPhone, or portable phone – (he referred to it as the *iPhone* with the "e" for "evil") – his silent invectives threatened to rise to a sonic boom when he saw the call was from Commissioner Edward Paul Lizzard III, Commissioner of Sandersonville Homeland Security. But as Lizzard was his supervisor – not his superior – Noonan had no choice but to take the call.

"Yes, (pause) sir. What can I do for you?"

Lizzard's voice was clipped, like this call was one he had to make, and the sooner it was over the better. (Noonan felt the same way but for a different reason.) "Something has come up, Noonan, that requires your immediate attention. Knowing how dedicated you are to the welfare of the department, I have re-scheduled the SCI for next week. This new assignment should be a breeze for a man of your talents."

"What talents are those, (pause) sir?"

"It seems that the United States Navy has lost a ship in our marina."

"Pardon?"

"Ship, Noonan, ship. A vehicle for travel upon the water."

"You mean it sank?"

"Captain Noonan, if it sank, the Navy would not be looking for it, would they?"

"I don't know, (pause) sir."

"No. It did not sink. It vanished. Poof. It entered the Sandersonville Marina, let off passengers and then disappeared."

"So it was a cruise liner?"

"No, a deep-sea fishing boat. I guess I lead you astray by saying *ship*."

"Why was the United States Navy following a deep-sea fishing rig?"

"Ours is not to wonder why, Captain, it is to support the mission of the Department of Homeland Security."

"Fair enough. (pause) Was there any particular reason for us to get involved? Crimes and vanishing on the sea are the purviews of the United States Coast Guard. Why are we even getting involved?"

"Well, it's a delicate situation. Hush-hush, you know, and all that, you understand."

"Actually, I don't."

"The Navy has reason to believe a smuggler was onboard. It's assumed he made it ashore and the boat sank."

"I thought you said the boat was missing and now you say it sank."

"I don't know, Captain." The Commissioner was clearly frustrated with Noonan's unwillingness to do what he was told. "All I know is what the Navy told me. One of their ships was shadowing a deep-sea fishing smack and lost it in the Sandersonville Marina. The Navy wants you to find it."

"Me?"

"'The 'Bearded Holmes,' they asked for you by name. Or, rather, your nickname."

"I guess it pays to advertise."

There was a lengthy pause on the line. Line, in this case, was a misnomer. It was an electronic connection, but still the tool of Satan which Noonan was required to carry on his person at all times as per the instructions of the self-styled high and mighty Commissioner of Homeland Security.

Noonan gave it one last try – not that he objected to being pulled from the SCI assignment even for one meeting. "But if it involves a crime on the water, the Sandersonville Police do not have jurisdiction."

"Captain Noonan! When the nation's security is at stake, jurisdiction does not matter. Just do it."

Then, blessedly, the line, electronic, went sail rabbit dead.

# CHAPTER 2

Every nook and cranny of the United States of America has its heartbeat. It is a pulsation unique to the neighborhood. And the throbbing comes and goes. Today, Little Italy in Manhattan is only three blocks along Mulberry Street. Before the turn of the last century, it reached as far south as Worth Street, west to Lafayette, east to the Bowery and north to Houston. Houston Street, not the city of Houston in Texas or any other city named Houston in 24 other states. At its zenith in size, Jacob Riis described Little Italy as the "foul core of New York's slums." Today it is an ethnic trip to yesteryear, a Neapolitan island in a multilingual city.

Coastal North Carolina communities are as different from the rest of the state as New Jersey is from New Mexico. Where men – Native and non-Native – have not dug up the dense underbrush and drained the swamps, the land is as wild as it was before the Lumbee wandered into the area a millennium and a half ago. Then there are the Outer Banks where big money began in butchering whales that had washed up on shore, looting sinking ships, and rum-running during Prohibition. During the Second World War, it was known as Torpedo Alley for the hundreds of American cargo vessels that went to the bottom of the sea courtesy of German submarines within a few miles of the North Carolina seacoast.

Oddly, while the Outer Banks are as far from Alaska as you can go and still speak English, the two areas have one very important idiosyncrasy in common. Both, in their own way, were nurseries for aviation. Even though the Wright brothers were from Ohio – a fact commemorated by Ohio license plates which proclaim the state the "Birthplace of Aviation" as opposed to the North Carolina license plate slogan, "First in Flight" – they, the Wright brothers, are credited with the first flight on December 17, 1903, in Kitty Hawk. While the history of flight thereafter in the lower states was not without drama and accidents, the story of aviation in Alaska was one of constant danger. To fly in Alaska before the era of LORAN and GPS was to take your life in your hands, even if your sojourn was a Sunday flight around Anchorage or Fairbanks. Alaska, indisputably, has the worst weather in North America over the ruggedest terrain in the Western Hemisphere. In the lower states, there are roads, cornfields, deserts and remote landing strips which can be used if something goes wrong while you are in the air. In Alaska, if something goes wrong, there is no Plan B. There is no place for an emergency landing. Just mountains and tundra. Alaskan pilots are the best in the world because they are still alive. As the old Alaska bush pilot expression goes, "There are old pilots and there are bold pilots, but there are no old, bold pilots."

Rodolpho Sacerdote was a child of both the Outer Banks and bush Alaska. Born in Manteo, he had learned to fly in Nags Head. He was a Coast Guard brat and when his father was transferred to Anchorage, Alaska, Sacerdote went with the family. He graduated from the old Anchorage High School, swept away when the oil money of the 1970s quadrupled the size of the city, and he was one of the first aviation graduates at the University of Alaska. He was the youngest pilot to run a commercial flying operation into remote fishing lodges along the 1,200 miles of the Aleutian Chain. He cut his teeth flying in whiteout conditions where LORAN was of little value and maps of no value. He survived more than a handful of crackups and only retired from the Aleutian run after he spent too many nights waking up with his clenched knuckles snowdrift white from gripping an imaginary joystick.

For the next three decades, his life went dark. He was off the grid. On purpose. There were three tours in Vietnam. He came with the Tet and was in the field the bulk of the time. He was in the Highlands, Cambodia and in a lot of places no one said the United States was fighting with troops where no one in Washington D. C. wanted to know we were fighting. Then he went from camouflage to camouflage, one of uniform color and the other of combat cover. He came out when the pay was better in Africa and then there was the Middle East. He was everywhere often and never on direct deposit to an American bank – or in his name.

But the world changed. Rather, politics changed. He didn't give up the game; the game left him. It became too organized, too bureaucratic, and there were too many eyes looking for his shoulder. He knew when it was time to go and he did.

But he was not through. He had a few more decades before he was in that ubiquitous rocking chair on the front porch watching the sunset. He had the front porch and the rocking chair. But he wasn't ready for the cushion and the sunset. Not yet. He had at least one more adventure in his blood. But it would take the right team. He had the scheme, not the timing.

Yet.

Then he was back.

By serendipity.

In this case, it rose from his roots. Both his Outer Banks and aviation roots. It was a celebration of the flight of the Wright brothers and the aviation world was coming to Kitty Hawk to pay their tribute. If you flew, wanted to fly, wrote about flying, or just wanted to rub elbows with the legendary cowboys and cowgirls of the sky, Kitty Hawk was the place to be that summer. It was to be ten days of aviation to rival Oshkosh. Everybody who was anyone in the aviation world would be there. For ten days, Kitty Hawk was going to the center of the aviation world – past, present and future. If you had wings on your soul, you were going to be in Kitty Hawk.

# CHAPTER 3

Navy whatever-rank-he-had Wynter Morales was not happy to see Noonan. Noonan did not know Navy ranks from species of apples at Costco. He knew Navy vessels no better. Probably called ships. Noonan caught up with the naval officer on a big ship – type unknown – just off the coast adjacent to the Sandersonville Marina. Noonan did not know beans about boats, ships or anything which floated and was larger than a canoe. He only knew three things about this naval vessel for sure: 1) it was big, 2) it was made of steel and 3) there were no holes in the hull because the ship was still afloat.

Noonan was escorted in something he knew as a powerboat to the naval vessel, which Noonan called a ship, and boarded the vessel being careful to look for life vests and lifeboats just in case the naval ship developed a leak. He saw neither. The ship had no rocking motion so Noonan was able to saunter along to the deck as he was being escorted to the Operations Room where Wynter Morales was drinking coffee and clearly cooling his heels. Wynter made his distaste clear before the two even shook hands. "Frankly, I don't have time for this Homeland Security cloak-and-dagger nonsense."

"You've been reading my mail." Noonan shook Wynter's hand and continued. "I've been ordered here by a higher authority."

"Then you have been reading my mail," Wynter said with a half-smile. "We both got booted into this by someone up the chain of command who didn't have to do the work."

"I call them 'the People of Show.'" Noonan smiled sardonically. "We do the work. They show up after the work's been and steal all the credit."

"Well," now Wynter was smiling, "seems we are in the same boat," he tapped the side of the Operations Room wall.

"Probably," said Noonan smiling. "All I know is the Navy lost a boat."

"W-w-e-e-l-l-l," it was a long 'w-e-l-l,' "That's not accurate. Let me start from the beginning."

"Fine. Just don't use Navy terms. I'm a landlubber and happy to be one."

Wynter liked that. "Two days ago, while on transit, . . ."

"What does 'while on transit' mean?"

Wynter smiled. "'While on transit' means we were on our way from Point A to Point B when we were called to special duty."

"An odd job."

"That's a nice way of putting it. Yes, sir."

"Forget the 'sir,'" Noonan said. "I'm Heinz until there's a crime scene."

"OK. Heinz. We were ordered into these waters to shadow a deep-sea fishing rig. Supposedly the rig was smuggling in one ton of gold. Our orders were to. . "

Noonan cut in. "Whoa! Isn't it the job of the United States Coast Guard to deal with crime on the waters of the United States and you cannot smuggle gold into the United States? It's legal to bring gold in."

"Yeah," snipped Wynter. "Exactly what I said but followed by a 'sir.' But I'm way down the chain of command. The lieutenant commander told the second in command who told the third in command who told me, so I got the job." He smiled. "I'm using landlubber words like you asked."

Noonan smiled.

Wynter continued. "I expressed concern . . ."

Noonan cut him off politely. "Let me guess. You were just told to 'do it.'"

"We're in the same boat, brother."

Noonan shook his head. "The stench of politics is gagging both of us."

"What we were told was a big-time smuggler was inbound. *Apparently,* the smuggler had a way to monitor the USCG communications network so the Coast Guard wanted the Navy to do the tracking. The Coast Guard is sort of public property, so they don't encrypt much. We also have more sophisticated tracking equipment."

"Is that reasonable?" Noonan shook his head. "I would have thought communication between and among Coast Guard ships and Navy ships would be secure when it comes to tracking a suspect ship. I meant, the Coast Guard goes after drug smugglers so I am sure their ship-to-ship the communication is in code or coded."

"They are."

"So what you were told was garbage."

"What a nice way to put it, yes."

"OK, now the gold. Where did it come from?"

"Later. At first we, as in I, was just asked to track the rig. We were able to decrypt the GPS fingerprint of the rig, and we just locked on. We followed the GPS into Sandersonville Marina."

"Did you ever actually see the rig?"

"Visually, no. Not with human eyes but we did lock-on. We were just following a GPS signal."

"OK."

"So we were sitting here when the rig went into the Marina. Then its GPS went ghost."

"So what? The rig was in the Marina. You were off the hook."

"You'd think so.

"I don't like the sound of this," Noonan said slowly. "Bad news is a'comin'."

"You got that right."

"A land patrol, and by that I mean a collection of you law enforcement folks on land, had a Search and Seizure for the rig, but they could not find it."

"I can understand that. I don't know boats so I'd have a hard time finding a specific boat in the Marina."

"I can understand that as well but I have to assume the land patrol was professional. They had all the time in the world so I am sure they did a thorough search. They found no boat that looked like the rig that had been washed or painted or had a name change. The rig was gone."

Noonan said something like "huh" and then, with a been-there-done-that tone, he said, "and you got blamed for either bad surveillance or general incompetence."

"That wasn't the worst of it. I, we," he waved his left hand about to imply the Naval vessel, "were accused of stealing a ton of gold off the rig, dragging it out to sea and giving the smuggler the deep six."

"Nice."

"Yeah. But the charge went to some regional Homeland Security wonk in Durham who shot the complaint to Washington D. C. who sent it to Naval Command who . . .'

Noonan finished the sentence. "And the 'solve this' order came down the Navy Chain of Command and it's sitting on your desk."

"Oh, it gets worse. I'm to coordinate on a daily basis with the nearest office of Homeland Security, Boris Hernandez, out of Manteo, who ordered me to work with the Sandersonville Commissioner of Homeland Security which, I believe, is your boss, this Edward Paul Lizzard."

"You've met?"

"No. He ordered me to work with you."

"And, of course, he said why."

"No, but I'm like you. I have a nose for the stench of politics. He sees a headline in it."

"For him, not us."

"Precisely. So, Captain Noonan, . . ."

"Heinz."

"So, Heinz, we're in this together, right up to nostrils."

"Well, Officer Morales, . . "

"If you're Heinz. I'm Wynter. With a 'y.'"

"With a 'y?'"

"With a 'y.'"

"Well, Wynter with a 'y,' we'll be wallowing together for a while. Let me see what you've got."

# CHAPTER 4

School buses are, quite literally, and in reality, identical. Inside and out. Even more important, they are invisible. Like taxi cabs in a large city. In New York, Philadelphia, San Francisco, and Atlanta, taxi cabs are a dime a dozen. It doesn't matter the color. Taxi cabs in Los Angeles are rare birds but in the other large cities, there are so many any specific one is 'invisible.' School buses, on the other hand, are invisible in all cities. There are so many of them they hardly deserve a glance.

Unless you are stuck behind one of them.

But, in most cases, they are simply impediments to travel, not noticeable like a blood-red Maserati or gold Rolls Royce. The buses wallow on the side streets of every city and town in America only attracting attention if you are waiting for your child to come off the bus. If you are not a parent – East Coast, West Coast, Northern Tier or Deep South –they are just orange behemoths with black lettering with stop signs which pop out like elephant ears every two or three blocks in neighborhoods. On the highways and byways, they are just orange whales with black letters going somewhere.

# CHAPTER 5

I t was a good day for ACTION FOR AMERICA. No, on second thought – and third – it was a great day! It was going so well it might have been planned. Maybe it was. Afterall, everyone knew Jesus was white. God was white too. Everyone knew that. You could see God himself on the ceiling of that chapel in Rome, whatever its name was. No one at the ACTION FOR AMERICA could remember the name much less pronounce it but, hey, everyone knew God himself, was white. And so as the first man. Adam. A white guy. Guaranteed! He was on the same ceiling in that church in Rome.

So, if God was white and Jesus was white, where did the burrheads get the idea that they were as good as the white man. Really?! Why didn't they read their history? Our history. The history of the United States of America. This was a white man's nation. Hey, they got imported! They didn't arrive on their own like honest white folk.

And the good news kept on coming. The statute of their patron saint – a white man – Confederate General Nathan Bedford Forrest, the first Grand Wizard, just had his day in court and won. He was going to stay up. On Confederate Avenue. So much for the proposed changing of the name of the street to "United Avenue." United? Unite what? Spooks, Jews, Catholics, and Whites in the same, same, same, united whatever. Those minorities should be happy they are allowed to make a living here in North Carolina.

The second and third bits of good news were linked. Dr. Alexander Lawson, the openly unapologetic white supremacist candidate for the Georgia State Senate, had come all the way to Turtle to address ACTION

FOR AMERICA. From Georgia! He was a hero! He had spent more than a year in prison in Georgia in a plot to kill Barak Obama, Barak Hussain Obama, that Kenyan upstart who fooled too many white folks into voting for a jigaboo. Well, people would learn. Obama was gone and a genuine white man had taken his place. 'bout time.

Lawson came with good news.

Even better.

He had a plan.

And, best of all, he was coming with cash. Plans are all well and good, you know, but money makes the world go 'round. With no money, plans are just, well, plans. Things you want to do and talk about doing but cannot do because, well you don't have the money to get started. With the money, you can make a statement. ACTION FOR AMERICA can actually live up to its name. No more just standing around with signs on street corners. There was enough money to make things happen. Big things, you know, that would get white Americans to realize just how close to the edge civilization is. Our civilization. The white civilization. The descendants of the Roman Empire. Some highly publicized actions here and there, and who knows, maybe white folk would realize the danger they were in. The danger we all in. Danger of Ebonics in the school, Sharia in the courtroom and statues with afros with cornrows from town square to the university. Jesus!

Now, with money, all things were possible.

# CHAPTER 6

Noonan took his coffee black and early. He only drank coffee after 1 p.m. when he was forced to suffer a *Naugahyde Night,* a night when he was sitting at a desk waiting for a lab test to conclude, a call from a far-off police station, fingerprints to match or a DNA smudge to find a parent. If there was no *Naugahyde Night* in his immediate future, he poured his last cup of Java at around 10 in the morning and was asleep by 10 in the evening.

Wynter did not seem to be affected by caffeine. But then again, Wynter might have been all of 40 years of age. Noonan was about to surge into the mid-seventies.

"Now, let me make sure I have this correctly," Noonan said as he pulled out one of his trademark note pads. "You got the call from a superior to . . ."

"Supervisor; not a superior."

Noonan smiled. "I hear you. You got a call from the Navy chain of command to shadow a deep-sea fishing rig into the Sandersonville Marina. Supposedly the rig was smuggling in one ton of gold."

"So far, so good."

"And the United States Coast Guard wasn't involved."

"Not as far as I know. I was told by Naval command the Coast Guard worried it would be spotted watching the vessel."

"But it would *not be suspicious* of a Navy vessel shadowing the deep-sea fishing boat? Seems a bit backward, don't you think?"

"You'd think so."

"I do. Odd, you know."

"Very odd."

There was a l-o-n-g moment of silence and then Wynter's verbal expression broke into asterisks. "Those ***** ***** ***** **** ****. We're being set-up, used."

"That's what I think too," Noonan said softly. "There is a very big game here, and we are being punched in as bit players."

# CHAPTER 7

Turtle, North Carolina, was named Turtle simply and necessarily because it started with the letter "T." There were turtles in the vicinity which made the new name a natural. There was also a regional high school in the city and one of the oldest small colleges in the state. The town had never been founded, *per se*, because it was like Topsy; it just grew up.

Turtle's original name had been Terminus though the community was never christened that way. It had been created at the confluence of three rail lines: north, south, and east. This was in the days before the automobile and plane. In the Golden Age of the Railroads, if you passed through North Carolina within 100 miles of the Atlantic, you necessarily passed through Terminus. It was laughing said wherever you were on the East Coast to wherever you were going to go, "you had to go through Terminus."

Terminus itself was nothing more than a massive switching yard with all the buildings, facilities, and accouterments that come from being a central railway hub: warehouses, mechanical sheds, tracks headed in all directions, switching stations, storage yards, and spur lines. All of these facilities and accouterments required workers, supervisors, and associated personnel and it was not long before a railroad town grew up around and along the confluence of tracks. Then came the inevitable: saloons, brothels, general stores and, eventually, churches, schools, and courts.

The community became large enough for two high schools and a small college. Since the city had no official name, it was just Terminus. The two high schools adopted the name for their athletic teams, and the small college had chess, debate and acapella clubs that competed across North Carolina. All teams and clubs used the word Terminus as their city of origin and the capital letter "T" as part of their logo.

Fast-forwarding to the 1930s, when the automobile and plane put many railroads out of business, Terminus collapsed as a railway hub. With roads, many of them paved, spider-webbing out across North Carolina and aircraft passing overhead, the community experienced death throes. What saved it was a cornucopia of small business opportunities. The Second World War brought a training camp to the hinterlands, and in the 1950s, tourism was a godsend. Farming had never been big in the area because the railway offered better jobs, but with the collapse of the railroad industry, agriculture began to make headway. Banking, automobile repair, insurance, gas stations, hotels, restaurants, and specialty stores replaced the decaying railroad structures and a dozen elementary schools erupted from the earth. The town was then renamed – or, originally named if you prefer – Turtle simply because it began with the letter "T," which was already the logo for the high school athletic teams and small college clubs.

So Turtle it became, another eye-scratching community between Greenville and Manteo with no particular claim to fame other than what it had been. Then, one day, unexpectedly, it became the focus of national attention when a school bus disappeared.

# CHAPTER 8

Harold and Jerrold were the Heckle and Jeckle of Turtle. Millennials will have a hard time connecting the two sets of twins because the later pair was off the television before most millennials were born. In the days before cable television. When you had four channels and you turned the tv on by pulling a knob. If you turned the knob, the sound level went up. And you could get a clearer picture by crawling onto your roof and adjusting the thin metal dowels on a pole called an *antenna*. (If you are a millennial, an *antenna* was something looking like a half-dozen metal shirt hangers on a stem that picked up television signals.)

Heckle and Jeckle, the television stars, were twin magpies who were always dealing with annoying adversaries. Though they were visual twins, they were not fraternal. One spoke with a British accent (Heckle?) and the other with a Brooklyn brogue (Jeckle?). (Or was it the other way around? No one knew because neither bird addressed the other by name.) The cartoons ran on television and as time-wasters in theaters for 20 years, from 1951 to 1971, about the time millennials started being born.

As an example of their antics, in "Thousand Mile Checkup," [Episode 47, which appeared in January of 1960, if you are so interested], the magpies had established the "Last Chance Service Station" in a remote spot along the roadway in the desert. Much to their dismay, a burly bulldog opened a competing station across the street and gas warfare began. Again, if you are a millennial, a 'gas war' was when two gas stations across the street from each other would drop the price per gallon to attract customers. One station would drop the price to say $.28 a gallon – keep in mind this was the 1960ss when gas was cheap – and the station across the street would drop the price per gallon to $.26. The original station would then drop the price to $.25 a gallon and the station across the street to $.24 a gallon. Drivers who loved gas wars would drive miles out of their way to get the cheap gas. The gas stations made up for the financial loss at the pump by having more people buying gas at the station. Or giving out 3x, 4x or 5x more Blue Chip or S&H stamps. [Millennials, ask your grandparents about Blue Chip and S&H stamps.]

In the on-screen 'gas war,' twins magpies and the bulldog blew up each other's gas stations, stole customers and even moved the stations closer and closer to the big city. One antic was to paint the bulldog's gas station like the roadway so a truck would 'drive though.' The episode finished with Heckle and Jeckle stuffing the bulldog into a gasoline hose and pumping him into a customer's tank. When the customer drove away, the bulldog went along the ride.

Harold and Jerold in Turtle, railroad engineers, were just as ingenious. They also had the same attitude. They had been born in Turtle in the days when the original tracks were being laid. They both had engineering degrees from the University of North Carolina when North Carolina was still a colony. They spent their days during the Second World War in Europe repairing train tracks, engines, flat cars, boxcars, fuel tank cars and military transport cars the German bombers had bombed all night. They jerry-rigged – today called jury-rigged – everything together all day only to see the Jerries, known today as the Germans – blow it apart all night.

At the end of the war, they returned to Turtle, where they became the jacks of all trades and all things having to do with tracks, engines, cars and, as the technology changed, the electronic doodads and programs which kept the railroads on life support while trucks and planes stole the industry blind. By the end of their careers, Turtle had been transformed from a massive transportation hub to a railroad ghost town. They were living uncomfortably on their pension in homes their parents had paid off in the Dark Ages. They referred to themselves as sourdoughs, 'sour' on Turtle but did not have the 'dough' to leave.

But they did know Jennifer Cartwright.

And she knew Rodolpho Sacerdote.

And they became one big, happy family.

# CHAPTER 9

Wynter was still cursing the gods when Noonan came at him sideways. "Ever hear of the Black-Spotted Sticky Frog?"

The statement took Wynter completely by surprise. "Where did that come from?"

"I have an insatiable intellectual curiosity," Noonan said without missing a beat – and as if Wynter was in breathless attention. "Everything interests me, (pause) and I am amazed how much animal behavior meshes with human nature."

Wynter gave a quick glance around the room to see if Noonan was speaking to someone else in the room. When it was clear he and Noonan were alone, Wynter asked, "Is this going somewhere?"

Noonan didn't miss a beat. "The Black-Spotted Sticky Frog is native to the Philippine Islands. It's quite small and when in danger, it emits a sticky secretion that is repulsive to its predators. Thus, its name."

"And?" Wynter let the question hang.

"There's more. What I find particularly academically fascinating about the Black-Spotted Sticky Frog is the unique way it protects its eggs. It lays them in a carnivorous plant, a pitcher plant. The eggs are beneath the surface of the plant's liquid so they are protected from insect predation."

Wynter took a moment to digest this fact. Then he said, "Let's see if I can predict where this is going. What you are saying, in your own way, is that Homeland Security isn't setting us up for failure. It's neutralizing us. Whatever those folks are planning, they want to be sure the most reasonable competing agencies are kept clear. It's not just keeping us in the dark. It's s keeping us off the field of play."

"Sort of. I'd say it's more like the administrative chain of Homeland Security is cooking up some scheme and wants all the credit. The best way to get all the credit is to keep every other department and agency, state and federal, in the dark. Homeland Security achieves that purpose by sending everyone who could be involved on wild goose chases."

Wynter chimed in. "And following your example of the Black-Spotted Sticky Frog, if anyone gets too close, they will find it unpleasant because Homeland Security has buried its plans deep in goo. That way no one is going to stumble onto its machinations."

"I'll live with your interpretation," Noonan smiled like a Dutch Uncle. "But there's more. The best way to keep the playing field clear for yourself is to have potential competitors squabbling. Having the Navy and the Coast Guard squabbling keeps them out of the fray. The local police, me," Noonan said tapping his chest, "is off chasing shadows and it will not be long before the North Carolina State Troopers are suckered into doing something time-consuming and pointless. That leaves the field open for Homeland Security to do its deed."

"Well, Homeland Security does not have the best and brightest working for them. I don't believe they could find chopsticks in a Chinese restaurant. Maybe we should just let them fail on their own."

"Good idea but not feasible," Noonan said as he furrowed his brow. "You see, if they try and fail, someone is going to have to take responsibility for the disaster. Homeland Security is a political organization, not a service one. It assigns blame. When it fails, it points the finger at people who cannot defend themselves. The United States Navy and the United States Coast Guard are not going to call Homeland Security a liar; they will just hope the press can figure it out."

"My impression of the press is not good."

"Most of the reporters are not very good, yes. They are just like every other profession. 90% of them are, at best, average. But there are 10% who are top-notch. Not all of them are asleep at the switch."

"Right now that doesn't do us any good. Let's put what we have on the table and see where we go from here."

"Not that much to put on the table," Noonan said as he tried to lean back in the military metal chair. He could not lean that far so he sat up straight. "So far we've pretty much have zip."

"You are right. We've got zip. We've got a story without a thread of believability. Worse, we're being asked to swallow it hook, line and sinker."

"Well, we don't want to disappoint anyone. So, for the moment, we've got to play a double game. First, we need to put enough effort into trying to solve this supposed crime, . . ."

". . . .without looking unbelievably stupid," cut in Wynter.

". . . without looking unbelievably stupid, yes," added Noonan right behind him, "While, at the same time, trying to figure out what the real game is and keep Homeland Security from screwing the pooch."

"What a nice way of putting it." Wynter paused for a moment. "You know, since you brought it up, I'm a bit of a scholar myself. What I know is not as exotic as the Black-Spotted Sticky Frog. Are you familiar with the German term *papierkrieg*?"

"No," replied Noonan with a smile. "But I'm always willing to learn."

"It translates as 'paper war.' It's when you get buried in paperwork to keep you away from a task. Like a court case where you have to keep responding to writs and motions whose sole intent is to frustrate you into dropping the matter."

"*Papierkrieg*. I like that bit of trivia. See, every day I learn something new."

"In this case, you'll get to live it. I've been in the Navy too long not know how to stall something. When someone higher up wants to *not* do something, they blizzard the scene with paper. Lots and lots of paper. I don't see us, that is, you and me, getting hit with a paper blizzard, but I do anticipate that we'll be sent on wild goose chase after wild goose chase to keep us from getting involved with what is really going on."

"I agree with you," Noonan shook his head sadly. "So, let's get the obvious out of the way first." Noonan smiled and shook his head sadly. "I'm betting the Coast Guard saw this for the dog it was and dumped it on the Navy."

"Been there; done that," Wynter said with a wry smile.

"I'm also betting the Coast Guard never even saw the fishing rig. I am sure they had the GPS. That's pretty easy to hack."

". . . even for the Coast Guard," Wynter said with a sardonic laugh.

"Now be nice," Noonan said shaking a finger at Wynter. "The Coast Guard's the first line of defense against drug smuggling by sea and the people they encounter are not friendly folk."

"Just a bit of interagency rivalry," Wynter added. "Some of my best friends are Coasties."

"They saved the Outer Banks for sure," Noonan said.

"OK, OK, enough niceties. We both agree the Coast Guard probably never set eyes on the fishing rig. It's easy to get the GPS and other electronics so that's what the Coasties passed on to us. Then they left chock-a-block."

"And," Noonan added, "since they never got a visual on the rig, they had no idea what color it was, what its name was, etcetera, etcetera."

"Right. So the boys in blue were looking for a fishing rig with no information. Ergo there was nothing to find because the information was bad."

"True," said Noonan and raised a cautionary finger. "But there is a cautionary wrinkle here. The GPS went ghost. That means it was turned off. Did that mean the people on the fishing rig knew they were being followed?"

"Wwweeeelllll," said Wynter dragging out the word and thought, "I'm a suspicious sort. I don't think the GPS went ghost – your term – on its own. It was shut off. Either someone on board was suspicious or just being safe. Either way we're dealing with some cagey customers."

"I agree," Noonan said nodding his head. "There is another tidbit to keep in mind. What I heard from my Commissioner was a hint at gold smuggling. In reality, there is no such thing. Having, transporting, or selling gold is legal. You cannot smuggle something legal. So why did the Commissioner mention gold? Was that a hint or a slip of the tongue?"

""Wwweeeelllll," said Wynter dragging out the word again. "If your Commissioner had the same IQ as mine, it was a slip of the tongue."

"I agree."

Wynter continued. "So, it gives the enterprise an added wrinkle. Whatever it is we are supposed to be investigating has gold associated with it."

"Actually, no." Noonan shook his head and left it cocked toward winter. "Whatever it is we are *not supposed to be investigating* is somehow associated with gold."

# CHAPTER 10

Contrary to what North Carolinians will tell you, no one is exactly sure why North Carolina is called the "Tar Heel State." While the derivation of the name is clear, its origin is not. During the Colonial period of American history, North Carolina was the world's leader in the production and exportation of tar, pitch, and turpentine. These were critical maritime building materials to the British Navy because the warm waters of the South Atlantic and Pacific had an abundance of shipworms. These animals, known as "termites of the sea," were a great danger to mariners. Growing up to six feet in length, the worms would bore into the wooden hulls of ships, pier pilings, and docks. The more worms, the faster the structure would deteriorate. But the ship-worms would not attack timbers treated with tar, pitch, or turpentine. Ergo, North Carolina become the world's leader in producing the three extracts. Before the American Revolution, North Carolina regularly shipped 100,000 barrels of tar and pitch to England each year. A century later, there were more than 1,600 turpentine distilleries in North Carolina and two-thirds of all turpentine in the United States came to North Carolina.

The origin of the term "Tar Heel" is shrouded in mystery. It is believed the term was originally a slur, the equivalent of 'poor, white trash' several generations later. Over the years, North Carolinians used the expression with pride. This sanitizing of a slur for publicity purposes became a North Carolina attribute. During the Presidential campaign of 1828, a native North Carolinian running for the highest office in the land, Andrew Jackson, was called a "jackass" by his opponent. Jackson liked the term and used its likeness on campaign posters. A generation later, political cartoonist Thomas Nast made the beast immortal in his drawings – though then, and today, it is referred to as the "donkey," not the jackass. As an interesting historical note, no one – including Andrew Jackson himself – was sure if he was actually born in North Carolina. He was born in the Waxhaws region of both North and South Carolina. The region had not been surveyed at the time of Jackson's birth, so, depending on the historical source, he might have been – or not – born in North Carolina. Only two other Presidents have been undisputedly born in North Carolina: James Knox Polk and Andrew Johnson. Interesting, considering the times of their presidency, one was a slaveholder who actually bought slaves while in the White House and the other was impeached and almost ejected from office for his compassionate approach to the South after the Civil War.

Returning the origin of the term "Tar Heel," it is alleged that the slur gained respectability during the Civil War when the North Carolina troops "stuck to their ranks like they had tar on their heels." Maybe. It has also been historically insinuated the term originated when North Carolina was reluctant to join the Confederacy. Then called "the reluctant state," the political joke making the rounds of the Southern states was

"Got any tar?"

"No, Jeff Davis has bought it all."

"What for?"

"To put (on North Carolinian soldiers) to make you stick."

Another apocryphal tale of the origin of "Tar Heel" came when the 4th Texas Infantry lost its flag in the Battle of Sharpsburg in Maryland. More commonly known as the Battle of Antietam, it was the bloodiest battle in both the Civil War and American history. The combined dead were 22,717. On September 17, 1862, Union General George McClellan hit Robert E. Lee's Army in the first clash between the two generals. The losses were so horrendous Lee ordered his army back to Virginia. McClellan failed to follow the retreating Confederates so Lincoln removed him from command. Returning to the origin of "Tar Heel," as the 4th Texas Infantry was passing the 6th North Carolina, a

Texan yelled a derogatory "Tar Heels!" and the North Carolinians and one replied, "If'n you had had some tar on your heels, you would have brought your flag back from Sharpsburg."

While the specific origin of the term "Tar Heel," is not known, the naming of the Tar River is not. It was an exit route for tar, thus the name, from eastern North Carolina. It runs almost 346 miles from its origin east of Roxboro and changes its name but not its waterflow when it passes under U.S. Highway 17 in Washington, North Carolina. Thereafter it is named the Pamlico River which, now brackish, feeds into Pamlico Sound.

It is said, and possibly true, that in March of 1862, as Confederate troops were abandoning Washington, North Carolina, they were ordered to burn all supplies which could be used by the invading army. There were 1,000 barrels of tar which they did not have the time to destroy so the metal hoops holding the wood staves in place were severed and the barrels rolled into the river. Three months later, several hundred Union prisoners were on their way to an exchange in Washington, North Carolina. The Union prisoners asked to be allowed to bathe in the river. Their request was granted. Their combined motions in the river brought the tar off the bottom and the prisoners came out of the water covered in tar. A Yankee soldier expressed his dismay in a statement which has become immortal: "We have heard of Tar River all our lives but never believed that there really was any such place, but damned if we haven't found it, the whole bed of it is tar!"

Rodolpho Sacerdote was well aware of the history of the Tar River. Even more important to him, its watershed was remote from the rest of the North Carolina yet, at the same time, was close enough to civilization he could live off-the-grid without having to live primitively. He had tried living off-the-grid in Alaska but getting food and supplies was so difficult even with a bush plane that off-the-grid was synonymous with survival. Not so down the Tar River. Supplies were available in Louisburg, Rocky Mount, Tarboro, and Greenville and one did not need an airplane – wheel or pontoon – to live off-the-grid in comfort.

Part of that comfort was aviation. Although he could not fly to his homestead – an Alaskan term for a homesite in North Carolina he had to buy with cash, not sweat – he did have a small plane in Greenville in which he indulged his aviation passion. Once every few weeks he could take his boat upriver and spend several days flying the skies of North Carolina, stopping on remote landing strips for no reason whatsoever. But over the years, he longed for something different. It was not as though he was looking for an improvement in his life, more creature comforts, a larger plane or an exotic vacation to the Bahamas. It was more he hungered for variety in his life. He was driven in the quest for *different*. He abhorred the same old/same old.

He was reaching a crisis point when he met an older woman taking flying lessons at the airport in Greenville, Jennifer Cartwright. She was from Turtle and suffered the same malaise. But, in her case, she had a lifestyle she wanted to leave with honor. She was caretaking a nephew with PTSD and his two infant daughters. It wasn't so much that she wanted the trio gone as much as she wished she could offer them a better future. Money would do it. But she had barely enough for the household – and the flying lessons: her mental relief. In Sacerdote she found a kindred spirit. And, as it turned out, much more.

# CHAPTER 11

Edward Paul Lizzard III and Boris Hernandez were huddled around a table piled four feet high with documents and dockets. Both men had burrowed out a canyon between them, the back gully connecting so they could speak without having to yell across the mountain range of paperwork.

"Well," said Lizzard with a broad smile as he tapped his iPhone off. "This is another fine mess we have gotten them into!"

Hernandez broke into uproarious laughter. Lizzard joined in with a high-pitched shriek of a laugh.

"Do you have even the remotest bit of remorse you are having your people running all over God's creation for nothing?"

"Oh, of course, I do." Lizzard pulled off his reading glasses and turned his head sideways. Then he pointed to the very corner of his right eye with the tip of his right glasses earpiece. "If you look very, very carefully, you will see a bit of glistening. If you don't recognize it, it's a tear. A tear of compassion."

"I have one of those too," chuckled Hernandez pointing at the back corner of his left eye with a ballpoint pen.

Both of them broke into uncontrollable laughter.

"This is going to be child's play," Lizzard said, tears of laughter streaming down his cheeks. "Who says we don't know what we're doing? All we have to do is sit tight and let these dimwit terrorists hang themselves. We'll swoop in at the last moment, snap on the cuffs and call the press. It can't be any easier than that."

"It isn't," retorted Hernandez. "The only stumbling block we have are the cops, Navy and Coast Guard. We don't need 'em, but we can't upset them. We just have to keep them busy. I can keep the Coast Guard offshore and that will keep them out of the game. Chasing ghosts, so to speak. The Navy can be kept out of the picture easily. All we have to do is keep them chasing their tails."

"True, true," mumbled Lizzard. "But the Sandersonville police are another matter. They're on the ground. They can't be ordered off a case. I've done the next best thing. I linked them at the hip with the Navy. You keep the Navy busy and that will keep my people busy too. Where the Navy goes, my people have to follow. Then, at the end of the day, when everything is revealed, we take the credit and everyone else will fight among themselves as to who gets the blame for missing the story of the century."

Hernandez patted himself on the back, "And all we have to do is send a few red herrings their way with a wild goose chase or too."

"Just as long as the goose isn't anywhere near the gold. I don't want anyone mucking up this finely-oiled caper. This one's for us; press, budget increases, a trip to the White House. We deserve it. We earned it. We've set the wheels in motion."

Hernandez suddenly became serious. "OK, setting the wheels in motion. You can start by sending your people to Sandersonville, Pamlico City, Buxton, and Hatteras on the Outer Banks to look for smugglers. Have them check on the fishing rigs. That'll take a few days. I'll have the Navy order their people to patrol offshore. They don't have to be told what to look for, just anything suspicious. I'll make it clear this is a Navy operation, not a JV with the Coast Guard. All we need here is about four days. Five days at the most. By the time anyone figures out what we've done.

"Well, if five days is all we need," and Lizzard quickly added, "at the most. I have the first red herring!" He waved a sheet of paper.

Hernandez smiled and pointed to a sheet to his left on the tabletop. "And I've got something *very special* for the United States Navy."

# CHAPTER 12

In the 1940s – and particularly in Europe – it was not uncommon for people to be multilingual. European immigrants to the United States often spoke three languages fluently: their mother tongue, a local dialect and French which was the universal language at that time. If there was one thing these immigrants had in common it was the consensus that American English was the hardest language to learn because there were no rules.

As an example, in Italian and French, every letter in a word is pronounced. Not so in American English. American English has words with letters that are not pronounced – knight, gnu, and government – words that are spelled the same way but pronounced differently – read, does, lead – along with words which sound the same but are spelled differently and have different meanings: too, to, two. Then there are words which are spelled the same and pronounced the same but have completely different meanings – dissipate – and collections of letters that spell words only if pronounced the way they appear in other words. For instance, there is the word "ghoti." The word is "fish" if one pronounces the "gh" is the "f" sound as found in the word "enough." The "o" is "i" sound as found in "women" and the "ti" is the "sh" sound as found in "nation." At the same time, there are words which have the letters in the same progression and combination but are pronounced differently, as in "quick" and "Buick." A few of the other American English linguistic duplicities include

1) The bandage was **wound** around the **wound.**
2) The farm was used to **produce**.

3) The dump was so full that it had to **refuse** more **refuse**.

4) We must **polish** the **Polish** furniture.

6) The soldier decided to **desert** his dessert in the **desert.**

7) Since there is no time like the **present**, he thought it was time to **present** the **present.**

8) A **bass** was painted on the head of the **bass** drum.

9) When shot at, the **dove** into the bushes.

10) I did not **object** to the **object.**

11) The insurance was **invalid** for the **invalid.**

12) There was a **row** among the oarsmen about how to **row** .

13) They were too **close** to the door to **close** it.

15) A seamstress and a **sewer** fell down into a **sewer** line.

16) To help with planting, the farmer taught his **sow** to **sow.**

17) The **wind** was too strong to **wind** the sail.

18) Upon seeing the **tear** in the painting I shed a **tear.**

19) I had to **subject** the **subject** to a series of tests.

20) How can I **intimate** this to my most **intimate** friend?

American English also has expressions which are concise in the United States but would take a paragraph to explain to a foreigner. A good example is "I would if I could but I can't so I won't." In other languages, "would' and "could" are the same word as are "can't" and "won't." But in American English, "would" and "could" as well as "can't" and "won't" have specific but subtle difference. Then there are words with two opposite meanings spelled the same way and pronounced the same way: *nonplussed*. One definition is "surprised and confused so much that [someone is] unsure how to react" and the other is "not disconcerted; unperturbed." And, of course, American English has phrases which are opposites yet have the same definition: "fat chance" and "slim chance."

A term that Jennifer Cartwright had come to accept as doubly duplicitous was the term "special education." First, it was both a euphemism and misnomer. Special education was neither special nor education. It was also not – euphemistically, really or reasonably – any of the other terms used to describe the individuals or teachers in the *industry:* special needs, aided education or exceptional education. Second, the participants were hindered from education normality by a variety of afflictions, none of their own choosing, euphemistically referred to as "learning disabilities, communication difficulties along with emotional and behavioral disorders." Then there were students with physical "difficulties" – another euphemism – for such merciless afflictions such as Cerebral Palsy, Muscular Dystrophy, and Spinal Bifida – and the spectrum of the blandly referred *developmental disabilities* which included Down's Syndrome.

Third, and most important, with proper counseling, medication, tracking, and competent parental participation, about half of the so-called special education students could lead reasonably normal lives and be a credit to their community.

History was in Jennifer's corner. One in every five humans on the planet has a form of mental illness, some clearly more pronounced than others. That being said, mental illness itself has never been a stumbling block to success. Abraham Lincoln and Charles Dickens suffered severe cases of depression. Ludwig von Beethoven and Winston Churchill were bipolar. Charles Darwin was agoraphobic, Michelangelo was autistic and Leonardo da Vinci had dyslexia. Many other famous people had individual quirks and eccentricities which were very odd or unusual but not sufficiently aberrant to lock them up, to use the parlance of their day. Balzac drank 50 cups of coffee a day, Dickens combed his hair as many as 100 times a day and John Quincy Adams swam nude in the Potomac every day at 5 a.m.

(As an historical aside, John Quincy Adams refused to meet with journalist Anne Royall so she waited until he went swimming. Then she sat on his clothes on the shore and refused to leave. She thus became the first female journalist to interview a sitting President of the United States – though, in this case, she was the one doing the sitting.)

It was Cartwright's considered opinion – an opinion for which no school board members had ever asked – about one-third of the so-called special education students were nothing more than cons. They did not want to expend the effort to read, write and do mathematics at the level of their peers so they "acted up" or "did not act their age." These individuals would be removed from the regular class and assigned to special education classes called 'Resource' where they would be coddled in the vain hope they would be wake up one day and be productive citizens – both a fat and slim chance.

Mainstreaming was successful enough to survive in the academic curriculum but there were a small percentage of individuals who would never be able to take care of themselves. They were going to be a burden to society for the rest of their lives. This was a reality in today's world as well as that of the ancient Egyptians, Greeks, Renaissance Italians, colonial Americans, Inupiat Eskimo, and Watusi. No culture is free of its helpless and hopeless.

Cartwright came to the world of special education through an odd side door. She was born and raised in a flyspeck of civilization, Hugo, Oklahoma. Even though its population had doubled since her birth, there were only a few more than 5,000 people living there in 2010. It was an odd town, even by American standards. For decades, it was known as Circus City USA because circuses spent the winters there. In fact, the Mount Olivet Cemetery in Hugo – known as Showman's Rest – hosts, so to speak, the remains of show people who spent their lives on the road. Some of the more notable residents therein include the original Marlboro Man, a Buster Brown midget and three world champion rodeo riders. The headstones include etchings of an elephant – not life-size – a circus big top – again, not life-size – and a wagon wheel monument to one Ted Bowman with lettering on the back reading "Nothing Left But Empty Popcorn Sacks and Wagon Tracks." For the living, during Cartwright's time in Hugo, it hosted the second-largest elephant herd in America – but only during the winter. Though small, Hugo is illustrious as it is the hometown of Bill Moyers, liberal political pundit and news personality and five-time Grammy Award winner B.J. Thomas, most famous for two songs, "Another Somebody Done Somebody Wrong Song" and the theme song from the film BUTCH CASSIDY AND THE SUNDANCE KID, "Raindrops Keep Falling On My Head."

In spite of all of this charm, Hugo did not have a lot of jobs. As soon as she graduated from high school, Cartwright headed for the big city, in this case, Broken Arrow. Even with a nursing degree, there were no jobs so she joined the Nurse Corps and spent three tours in field hospitals in Vietnam with names she could pronounce but left most Americans tongue-tied. After the fall of Saigon, she bounced across America through a laundry list of hospitals, most of whom wanted younger nurses. She finally found her niche in Turtle where she filled a joint position with Turtle General Hospital and the Turtle School District. As the two facilities were within walking distance, she could do double-duty which pleased both employers because she was half-time in both, had her health care covered by Turtle General and her retirement by Social Security.

She was particularly valuable to the Turtle School District because she was medically equipped to handle special education. She was intimate with the pharmaceuticals taken by the kiddos – as they were called by the administration at the Turtle School District office complex of four rooms – as well as the individual reactions to those drugs as the kiddos grew and matured. In the classroom, she was patient, understanding and was unaffected by behavior difficulties and the wide range of physical, mental, and psychological afflictions of the kiddos.

She had never needed much money and she had relationships which were as frequent and long as needed to keep her hormones in check.

Then came 2008 and her home lost half its value in the subprime mortgage disaster.

Then a nephew with PTSD from the Iraq War moved in with his two daughters because they had no other place else to go.

And the Turtle School District cut back on her hours.

And one day Rodolpho Sacerdote told her of a plan he had been percolating for years.

# CHAPTER 13

Archie Scarborough was an old hand at magic tricks. He had made his living as a magician. For a while. At one time. As a traveling magician rather than a regular gig in Atlantic City, Las Vegas, or the Catskills. It had been a good living – but nothing to brag about. He traveled a lot, about 100 days a year, all expenses paid.

But it got old.

He loved the ocean – rather, he loved the oceanfront at his front door – therefore to settle too far from saltwater made him jumpy. So he settled on the coast of North Carolina; Manteo as his place of residence. He still traveled, of course. The magic money was too good to give up and, frankly, Scarborough's Theatrical Emporium in Manteo was not a moneymaker. It made for a retirement income but not much more.

He was still 'in the magic field,' so to speak, so he was always thinking of new tricks. He had also been in the magic field long enough to know there was always someone looking over your shoulder. Mostly other magicians looking for 'the next new thing' and most of them were not smart enough to boil water. Since they could not originate tricks, they stole them.

To keep his 'tricks of the trade' secret, Scarborough went to great lengths to hide both his stage props and preparations. Keeping the stage props secret was easy. He, as with most magicians, went to great length to keep the props and presentations as mysterious as possible.

From the audience side.

But it was a Herculean chore to keep the stage side preparations secret. This included whisking away any clues as to how his tricks were done, even the most elementary. There was always an up-and-coming magician who found it easier to steal someone else's thunder rather than make their own.

To keep it a secret – even a hint – of what his next trick was going to be, Scarborough eschewed shopping in magic stores. *Eschewed*, though a rare word, describes precisely what he did. The magic community was small and, like a small town, everyone knew everyone else's business. In the case of his industry, everyone else's tricks. So, when he went shopping for the ingredients for his next bolt of lightning (on stage), he perambulated to non-magic stores. And his perambulations were not confined to any one city. He never shopped for his raw materials on the Outer Banks and rarely inland. He went north, to Virginia Beach, Norfolk, Richmond, and even Washington D. C.

To further confuse the competition, he never bought everything he needed for one trick in the same emporium. Sometimes he even split the order to keep any prying eyes from knowing what he had planned. He also bought red herring bits and pieces to confuse any of those prying eyes. If someone were following him, all they would get was a laundry list of items he had bought of which, maybe, one-third were actually going to be used on stage. Whether it was cables or curtains, plexiglass for a water tank, balsa wood, paint, metal cables, ropes, plastic balls, or even a top hat complete with a rabbit compartment, he left it a mystery, so to speak, as to what he was going to do. Prying eyes, you know, and everyone in the magic business was watching everyone else all the time. That was the business so it made sense to cover your trail.

# CHAPTER 14

Noonan tapped the "Call End" red circle on his tool of Satan and waited until the face of the iPhone went back to its standard.

"Let me guess," said Wynter reading Noonan's face like a book. "You've got your first run-around-like-a-chicken-with-its-head-cut-off assignment."

Noonan gave a sardonic smile. "Well, we were expecting it. I'm betting you'll get your call really soon."

"What a joy," Wynter said with an acerbic smile.

"Before we go our separate ways on wild goose hunts, we need to coordinate what we have to do. If I am telling you something you already know, let me apologize in advance."

"No apologies necessary. We need a plan of action." Wynter replied.

"OK, we have to do at least three things at the same time. First, we have to do what we are ordered to do no matter how meaningless it is. At the same time, we have to do it as s-l-o-w-l-y as possible. This will give us the time to do the undercover work we need to do to figure out what is really happening. And, I hate to say it, at the same time we will prove to Homeland Security that we are the bumbling idiots they think we are."

Wynter gave a wide grin. "Doing something s-l-o-w-l-y is a Navy specialty."

"Second, we need to know what is going on. Really going on. Which means we have to cautiously work our way back up the chain of command that got us here and see if there is anything we weren't told originally. Any tidbit could be important. Third, we need to follow the only lead we have – if it is a lead at all. The gold. For some reason this has something to do with gold."

Wynter agreed. "Sounds like a plan. Let me take the lead on the gold. If you nose around everyone is going to assume that it has something to do with a crime and then things will get all balled up. I am sure you know when the cops show up, everyone gets really quiet while the cops are there and then talk up a storm afterward. Or they ask for things like warrants and subpoenas. Cops cannot be subtle. Stupid Navy people," Wynter pointed at his face and stretched a stupid grin across his face, "can ask dumb questions without raising any suspicion."

"Sounds like a plan to me," Noonan replied. "We've got to be as subtle as possible to pull this off. The bad news is we're only going to get one shot at this. The minute anyone figures out what we are really doing we will be out of the game completely." Noonan took a breath. "I'll see what I can dig out of Homeland Security in Sandersonville. But I need you to get back with the Coast Guard. They are the ones who got the original complaint . . ."

". . . and dumped it on the Navy. Yeah, I can do that. Better that it come from me than you."

"No time for a landlubber, eh?"

"No. Lack of patience with a landlubber. I'm sure it's the same with the cops, er, your department. When everyday citizens stop by to ask a question, it's not a joy. It's a waste of time."

Noonan was silent as he pulled a business card from his wallet. He flipped it over and started to write on the back. "This is my cell number. Only two people have the number, my wife and the Sandersonville Commissioner of Homeland Security." He finished writing and handed Wynter the piece of paper. Wynter responded with a card of his own.

"I'm not married but I get calls from friends. And supervisors. And my parents. And salespeople. And . . ."

"I get your point. Get a disposable phone. If and when we need to talk, I need to reach you and not have my message lost among . . ."

"Got it. I'll get a disposable phone and call you," he waved Noonan's business card, "and let you know the number. Now, what was your waste-of-time assignment?"

"Actually, it's a good and bad assignment. I am to double-check all boats at all marinas and tie-ups in Sandersonville, Buxton, and Hatteras to make sure all boats are accounted for. And, specifically, to see if I can identify the missing fishing boat."

"Seems like a lot of work. What's the good news?"

"The boat we are looking for has to have a charter permit. Those boats must register with the State of North Carolina. All I have to do is get a computerized list of charter owners and focus on Sandersonville, Pamlico City, Buxton, and Hatteras. If I'm lucky, those charters had to log in and log out. If I am really, lucky, I can do everything I'm required with a few phone calls."

"Yes," said Wynter with a Machiavellian smile, "but that's going to take, say, two or three days."

"Absolutely. Full-time for two or three days."

"Just keep those phone calls going into your Commissioner so he doesn't realize what a nothing assignment he gave you."

Noonan gave a grunt and pointed at Wynter. "I can hardly wait to hear what joyous challenge your people have for you?"

"Oh, I'm sure it will be an anchor watch for sure."

"Eh?"

"'Anchor Watch.' It's a euphemism in the Navy for standing around and doing nothing. Watching the anchor. Anchors are only used. . . ."

"I got it." Noonan said. "Anchors, as in what you throw out when you need it and take in when you don't."

"I've never heard that."

"Tell a friend. In our case, to use another nautical expression, we now have to start shuffling deck chairs on the **Titanic.**"

"Considering the talent of Homeland Security thus far, we could very well be on the **Titanic.**"

Noonan smiled. "OK. Enough of the light talk. Now, for the moment," he held up his cell phone, "we should not be using these. We'll have to go low-tech for the moment. Use the landline to my office." Noonan dug in his pocket and pulled out a crumpled business card.

"You don't pass out a lot of these cards do you," Wynter said as he held the card between his thumb and forefinger.

"Crooks don't want them; bosses don't need them and no one ever asks for them."

"I wonder why," Wynter said as he put the card in his breast pocket. "Until I get a disposable cell phone, we'll have to use the phone number I have. " He put his right index finger to his lip, "mum's the word."

"Mum's the word," Noonan repeated as he put a scrap of paper with Wynter's phone number in his pocket.

# CHAPTER 15

Michael Patterson of Patterson Precious Metals in Manteo was used to the voice on the phone. He looked forward to it. It was, quite simply, money in the bank. His business, like every other precious metal operation, lived-and-died by the Law of Supply and Demand. When the price of gold was up, he was happy. When the price of gold was down, his family ate hot dogs instead of rib-eye steak. (It wasn't quite that bad; that was just the excuse he used when his two boys wanted a raise in their allowance.)

Boris Hernandez was good news to Michael Patterson. Whatever it was that Homeland Security wanted with 800 pounds of gold was fine with Patterson. He was the one selling the 800 pounds of gold. Better yet, it was an across-the-counter sale. No discount required! He was just to accumulate the gold until it reached the 800-pound figure. Then he would pick up the phone and call Homeland Security. It would send an armored truck to pick up the gold and that would be that. No transportation costs to Patterson Precious metals!

Even better, pound after pound, the government checks from Homeland Security were clearing.

What was Homeland Security going to do with 800 pounds of gold?

Patterson did not know.

Patterson did not care.

Patterson was in business to make a profit and Homeland Security was just like any other customer who came walking through his front door. There was nothing illegal about Homeland Security buying gold and their money was good. Even more important, every check he had received had cleared. That was America at its finest!

# CHAPTER 16

If you want to start a business, any business, there are five critical considerations:
1. Do you have something to sell?
2. Is there someone willing to buy what you have to sell?
3. Is there a communication system in place between seller and buyer?
4. Is there a transportation system in place between seller and buyer?
5. Is there a banking system in place between seller and buyer?

To be successful, every one of these considerations must be under your control. If they are, your business has a chance of surviving. Until one of the considerations changes and then, as the expression goes, 'you are back to square one.'

In the early days of the American republic, money – as in the actual pieces of paper – was the determining factor in the survival of a business, family and, for that matter, a nation. When the United States Constitution was written, the founding fathers purposely left a void for banking. Banking was not written into the Constitution so the United States, unlike England, for example, does not have a national bank. Thereafter, courtesy of the Tenth Amendment, the power of banking was left to the states.

Things did not go well.

In fact, when it came to money – again, the actual pieces of paper – things did not go well until the United States came off the gold standard in 1933. The first stab at a national currency came just before the Civil War when Abraham Lincoln's Treasury Secretary, Salmon Chase, ordered the first printing of United States paper currency. (Yes, his first name really was Salmon, just like the fish.) The paper currency was green and thus originated the term "greenbacks" for money. Until 1945, Chase's portrait appeared on the U.S. $10,000 bill. After that, the $10,000 bills were removed from circulation.

The printing of greenbacks was critical to the Union war effort. Before the greenbacks, paper money was printed by banks. Prior to the Civil War, states would authorize a bank to form. That bank would open for business and take in gold as a deposit. When the depositor wanted some walk-around-cash, he/she was given paper money printed by the bank where the gold was deposited. This was all fine-and-good if the depositor wanted to spend those dollars geographically close to the bank. But the further the purchaser was from the bank of deposit, the less likely the paper dollars would be accepted. The United States Army could not afford to be left without supplies in Philadelphia, for instance, if all the Quartermaster had in Philadelphia were paper dollars printed by a New York bank. Salmon Chase solved the problem by establishing a national currency.

But that still left the 'small investor' without an option. If you were a farmer in Iowa and wanted to sell your corn to a buyer in New York, how did you get your money? The buyer was not going to send the money in cash. And a New York check had no value in Indiana. Making a long story short, this was the origin of American Express founded by Henry Wells and William G. Fargo. Fargo died in 1881 and was replaced by his brother, James Congdell Strong Fargo.

While things were going well for American Express in the United States, the same could not be said about Europe. When James Fargo went to Europe on business in 1890, he went with Letters of Credit. From a United States company. Few Europeans would accept the Letters of Credit so Fargo was consistently short of money. When he returned to the United States, he lamented this sad state of affairs to an employee, Marcellus Flemming Berry. Berry was a nuts-and-bolts genius – now known as the "Edison of Finance" – and he had an idea. A very good one, as a matter of fact. Rather than go to Europe with Letters of Credit, why not go with blank checks? Then, when you needed money, you could show the bank clerk a piece of identification with your signature and then sign the check in the clerk's presence. You did not have to be a handwriting genius to see if the two signatures matched. Thus was born the American Express check.

Rodolpho Sacerdote understood the power of paper. Money was paper but it was really just printed paper. It was the faith in that piece of printed paper that gave it power. You could take a $100 bill, a piece of paper, into a store and come away with $100 work of real goods: apples, oranges, coffee, cream, meat, and potatoes. That was not because the paper was worth $100 but because the store had $100 worth of faith in the piece of paper.

Coming up with a false identity was easy. As long as you did not overdo it. The more you wanted to do with the false identity, the riskier it got. He only needed one false identity. And he only needed it for a short period of time. Even more important, he only needed it for a woman in her sixties. These were the easiest of identities to create. People are naturally trusting of an older woman. Young people, men or women, were suspicious characters. Particularly if money was involved. Those people got the double-check. Not so much a matron.

Jennifer Cartwright looked the matron.

Over the years, Sacerdote had worked for seedy taverns and night-clubs. Primarily because they were the kind of places he preferred. They were off-the-grid when it came to the paperwork trails, they paid in cash and asked very few questions. As long as you did not have a criminal record, you were hired. When he finally made the decision to settle in North Carolina, he was still working as a doorman and bouncer in Ashville, Wilmington, Raleigh, and Winston-Salem. Ever the opportunist, when he gave someone the boot for being underage, he, by State of North Carolina law, pulled their fake identifications out of circulation. But he did not destroy the cards. He kept them. Just in case, you know, if he should ever need one.

Now he did.

So he went through his collection. Most of the cards were so obviously bogus they were unusable. Those which remained were old. But that, to a creative thinking like Sacerdote, made them usable. In most cases, the cards seized had been because a Julie tried to use her older sister's ID and it failed. So the card was seized and the older sister had to get another driver's license. Now, ten years later, Sacerdote still had the North Carolina driver's license. It had expired, of course, but the format of the license had not changed. Now it was simply of matter of upgrading the license to the present day.

That was easy. A quick check of the North Carolina Voter Registration list gave Sacerdote Julie's older sister's current address. Then he removed the lamination over the old driver's license and replaced the portrait with one of Jennifer Cartwright. (Who really looks like their driver's license picture?) With photoshop he put in the new address, jiggled the expiration date, replaced the lamination – the old lamination, not a new sheet because that would have been a dead giveaway – and spent a day and half stomping on the card to give it a well-used look. With the card, Jennifer Cartwright got a Post Office box for a gift shop. Then she got a business license for the gift shop – for all of $50 – with the Post Office box as the address of record. She used the business license to open a bank account. Then she became making regular, small cash deposits to the account and wrote checks for services expected for a small business: rental, office supplies, inventory and cleaning services. All checks cleared because there was money in the bank to cover the expenses but no one in the bank seemed to notice that all of the expenses were billed to other businesses with Post Office boxes for an address.

# CHAPTER 17

It was mid-afternoon when Noonan got a phone call – on his landline – from Wynter. Yes, Wynter had received his 'sweep the horizon' assignment.

Noonan, cautiously, answered the phone professionally. As a civil servant, he did not have the option of ignoring incoming calls on the official line – even though he usually got crank calls.

With the exception of those from Sandersonville Commissioner of Homeland Security Edward Paul Lizzard III.

"Noonan."

"Wynter here. Are you sure this is a secure line?"

"No one listens to incoming police calls. They are boring. Whacha got?"

"I did get the call to spin my wheels. Unfortunately, I got the call. Fortunately, it came from Navy headquarters ordering me to coordinate with Boris Hernandez, Coastal North Carolina Commissioner of Homeland Security."

"Are there that many commissioners of Homeland Security?"

"Where there is federal money, there are federal employees. You should know that by now!" Wynter chuckled.

"Yes, you are correct. Both of them."

"Both of them?"

"More money means more employees and I should know that by now."

Wynter turned serious. "I'll have to think about what you said, (pause), but not right now. As we suspected, I got my marching orders."

"Let me guess, it's a time-wasting exercise in futility."

"Yup. But the commissioners made a slip. One of two things happened. First, since the commissioners of homeland security are political appointees and not professionals . . ."

"You can say that again," Noonan sniped.

"I agree." Then Wynter continued. "Because they are political animals they see the world through their own lenses. They have had unbelievable problems in dealing with the bureaucracy so they assume we will too. But we deal with the bureaucrats every day, so we have a lot of end-around-runs."

"So, let me guess." Noonan mused. "You were given an assignment they believe is going to take 872.4 hours when, in fact, it will only take a wily fellow like you a few hours to complete."

"Even faster than that. And even better than that, it has to do with gold."

That statement took Noonan by surprise. "It has to do with gold? They slipped up by mentioning gold in the initial contact with you and now you are given an assignment having something to do with gold?"

"Right. And because the assignment is connected with gold, it means I can nose around and not be suspected of upsetting the apple cart."

"Oh, that is delicious," Noonan chuckled. "And what is this solid gold assignment you that has been dropped on your doorstep?"

"All gold coming into the United States is legal but it still has to be declared. If someone is bringing more than $10,000 in gold, that's about eight ounces at today's prices, that someone has to fill out a form. FinCen Form 105."

"FinCen? Financial Crimes people in the Department of Treasury?" Noonan's face showed a visceral reaction to FinCEN. "I've dealt with those people before. They are neither the best nor the brightest."

"Every bureaucracy has idiots," Wynter laughed. "Navy's got lots of them. Don't judge the entire agency by one or two stumblebums. I don't judge the Sandersonville Police Department by the superintendent who also happens to be the Sandersonville Commissioner of Homeland Security."

"Got a point there," Noonan said as he reached for his pen and notebook. "Whacha got?"

"I have to give you some background first. Like I said, it's perfectly legal to bring gold into the country as long as you declare it."

"If it's more than $10,000 worth," Noonan added.

"Right. If it's over $10,000 worth you have to fill out FinCEN Form 105. The form is then sent to the United States Department of Treasury in Washington D. C., where it is filed away. What is used for I do not know. I'm assuming that the names from the form are matched with known drug dealers, traffickers, whatever, to see if there is a link. Other than that, the forms and the information on them just sit in D. C."

"And this has to do with you . . ." Noonan prodded Wynter.

"I have been instructed to coordinate with the Coast Guard to get a list of all people and companies who brought gold into North Carolina."

"That's stupid," Noonan said quickly. "You can trace gold when it comes into the United States, but after it gets here, where it ends up in anyone's guess."

"Yup. The only reliable information about incoming gold is with FinCen in Washington D. C."

Noonan was silent for a moment. "I must be missing something here. You are being ordered to get a list of names of people who brought gold into the United States from FinCEN and that list already exists?"

"Yup, again. Here's what I think is happening. The two geniuses of Homeland Security believe I am going to be jumping through bureaucratic hoops and stumbling into roadblocks for weeks to get that list. They are assuming I will send the request up the Navy chain of command who will forward the request to the Coast Guard which has its chain of command. Then the request will move it up the chain of command at the Department of Treasury and then, believe it or not, to Homeland Security. The United States Coast Guard is under the Department of Homeland Security."

Noonan shook his head, "So even if it makes it up the chain of command, the request is going to come right back to Lizzard and Hernandez for approval. Talk about the 'long and winding road.'"

"Beatles. Your generation." Wynter required. "Mine was 'a whole bunch of nothing.'"

Noonan smiled. "Which means there will be no response until long after whatever is supposed to happen does happen."

"More likely, nothing will happen. The request will simply disappear."

"So you have been assigned to spin your wheels waiting for a line of command people to get off their . ." Noonan did not finish the statement.

Wynter chuckled. "That's what they think, (pause), and I have no reason to convince them otherwise."

"And you have a plan?"

"Of course! I've played this game before! You dodge the chain of command. I wrote a Coast Guard Commander I know and asked him for the FinCEN list for North Carolina. He wrote me back that FinCEN files are in the Department of the Treasury, so ask them. I now have a written document from the Coast Guard that I coordinated with Coast Guard. I was ordered to coordinate with the Coast Guard and I have."

"C-l-e-v-e-r. You could probably only do that in a large operation."

"The larger the operation, the more ways there are to plow around the stumps."

"OK, so that solves the Coast Guard problem. Now you have to deal with the FinCEN people in D. C."

"Sort of. Like I said, I've played this game before. I call it the 'power of the pint.'"

"'Power of pint.' Nice alliteration. I like it. Tell me about the 'power of the pint.'"

"What the Commissioner of Homeland Security for Coastal North Carolina expects me to do is use the chain of command in place. That's because he's a political appointee and he's used to looking *down* the chain for command. He has no idea who is at the bottom of the chain of command. He wants something to happen so he sends instructions down the chain of command. At the bottom of that chain of command are we, the people who have to carry out the ridiculous orders. But we have our way of doing things. If we do it the way the political appointees want it done, nothing will ever get done."

"Which," Noonan cut in, "is the way the top dogs want it done to waste a lot of the time."

"Granted," Wynter replied. "But when something has to get done, we at the bottom have our own methods. That's where the 'power of the pint' comes in. I do not use the chain of command. I call around to competent people I have worked with in the past and ask for contacts within the Department of Treasury who are reasonable. I get a name, make a call and suggest we have a glass of beer at an out-of-the-way tavern. As long as what I am asking is reasonable, I get what I want."

"And someday you will return the favor," Noonan added.

"Exactly," Wynter replied. "Sooner or later I will get a call from someone I know saying I should contact so and so for a favor. It's done every day."

"But if you went through the chain of command, you'd be spinning your wheels for weeks."

Wynter laughed. "That's the way the federal government works. There are the political people who want their names in the paper and the worker bees."

"I call them the people of sweat and the people of show. Same thing."

"Well, we're the people of sweat. I just wanted to give you a heads up that I'll be in D. C. for a few hours. Just long enough for a pint of beer."

"Meeting with someone from Treasury who . . ."

Wynter cut him off. "For my health, Heinz. For my health. Who knows what I will come back with? Besides, don't you know, FinCen Form 105 is a public document. You just have to know the right people."

"It's amazing what a pint of beer will do. Just don't tell the . . ."

". . . Commissioner of Homeland Security for Coastal North Carolina? Of course not! He expects me to use the chain of command, so being the dutiful officer I am, I followed his orders. I sent an official letter to the Commandant of the United States Coast Guard and the Secretary of Homeland Security asking for their assistance in providing a list of FinCEN Form 105s for North Carolina."

"And you sent a copy to the Commissioner?"

"Of course. I want him to think I'm spinning my wheels."

"Clever boy."

"I'll make a phone call a day and send a progress memo every few days to the Commissioner. No reason to let him *worry* that I'm not on the job."

"Oh, but you are devious. What do you think you'll find in the FinCen Form 105 documents?"

"Butkis. A. If there were anything to find I would not have been given the assignment. B. This is a make-work project so the assignment was made to keep me off the field of play. C. Right now, the commissioners think we are both up to our ear lobes chasing paperwork. They don't know we'll clear the decks in a few hours. All we have to do is keep reporting progress. Or, in our cases, lack of progress. That'll keep them off our backs."

# CHAPTER 18

There are some word combinations that frighten humans to their core: child oncology, mercy killing, and Cerebral Palsy. Every prospective parent expects a boy or a girl. They can cheat, so to speak, with an ultrasound but, in most cases, parents only want a boy or girl preceded by the adjective "healthy." No parent expects a less-than-normal child. No parent wants a less-than-normal child. If they get one, their life will change instantly—forever.

Abdula Channing was born with Cerebral Palsy. She would never be normal by any stretching of the definition. Nicely put, she suffered from the neurological disorder brought about by a non-progressive brain malformation. That aside, her parents loved her very much. But her peers did not. She was a pariah in her neighborhood and at school. She was one of *them*, those segregated because of a physical or mental affliction. None of *them* would ever grow up to be good citizens who got a job, raised a family, paid taxes, attended church regularly, and volunteered for some social service nonprofit. *They* were going to be a burden to society forever – financial, social, and spiritual. *They* made it hard to remember you were a good Christian.

She had never known life without being seated: wheelchair, bed or toilet. She did not speak except in grunts and fought when her parents tried to dress her. She drooled and had to have her nose cleaned, and bottom wiped after a frequent visit to the toilet. She was only blessed inthat she did not recognize the disdainful looks of adults and children alike at her condition.

Jerome Abramowitz was blind and autistic. He had no concept of Tuesday or noon. Even though he was fed on a regular basis, every meal was a surprise. He took his pills because they were mixed with his food. If he tasted his food, no one knew. His communication was limited to silence and he spent most of his day playing with water beads, splashing them to and fro in the large plastic bin in the Special Education room. The Special Education assistants had to keep a sharp eye on Jerome Abramowitz because he had no sense of bathroom time. When it came time to evacuate, he did.

Darius Abd Al-Quadir was the most consistently articulate of the kiddos. But this was not saying much. He was articulate in the sense he formed words that sometimes were coherent in sentences. This is not to say he was transmitting information with the words which he spoke. Most of the time he was in Special Education he sat in a lawn chair and speaking long strings of words to no one in particular and unconcerned if anyone was listening. His words were in both English and Arabic but were unconnected in any logical or coherent order. His presence was blessed by the Special Education assistants because he had a sense of internal bowel signals and would move for the bathroom when such movements were pressing on his intestinal canal. On the downside, he could explode into a frenzy of dashing around or throwing stuffed animals, plastic dishes, and/or lunches without advance notice. He could and would bite without advance notice as well.

Shelia Mugavi was blind. She was also the survivor of some virulent childhood virus that had rotted her brain stem to the point her maturity stalled at seven or eight years of age. She was 12 now and was as compliant as the plastic dolls in the toy containers in the Special Education room. She spoke frequently but what she said had no connection to any person, event, or incident around which she was associated. She spent most of her day rolling about on a six-foot diameter dog poof jammed into a corner to keep her from rolling off and around on the floor.

Camilla Sanchez was normal in the sense that she realized her biological needs. She alerted the Special Education assistants when her bladder or bowels needed emptying. She ate when served, took her pills when offered and slept when it got dark. She had no concept of parents other than people who took her to the bus and retrieved her later though she had no sense of time passing. She was compliant but nonresponsive other than basic physical needs.

Then there was Chloe Adrondak.

Adrondak was a con.

Yes, she was a Special Education person in the sense that she could not be in a normal classroom setting, but she was a whiner, thief, and fabricator of the first order. Nothing she said could be taken at face value and she, among the other five, was the most articulate when it came to complete, understandable sentences. But being articulate did not mean she made any sense. That is to say, her sentences were complete and the words linked but the thoughts behind those words were not designed for communication. They were designed to mislead. She detailed conversations she had with ghosts, lied about what her parents said was good for her at school and swore she had taken her medication even though the medication she was to take was still in the hands of the Special Education assistant. She was constantly trying to make her escape by testing every door and window lock on a regular basis. She stole for no reason, ate her lunch and then said someone else had stolen it so she could get a second helping, publicly urinated if no one listened to her rants and used her feces as items to throw rather than flush.

Six kiddos. They were a handful. But the four Special Education assistants Jennifer Cartwright had hired were making very good money. Because of the unique nature of their assignment, Cartwright was paying three times the normal daily rate. The four assistants, from Wilmington, Tarboro, Charlotte, and Durham, had never met each other. They had all been contacted by Cartwright by word of mouth through professional contacts. It was a good gig. A seven-day job to take care of six kiddos in a secure location. Supposedly their collective parents were on a professional holiday and the kiddos needed to be looked after 24/7. There were some unique requirements to the job but not of any great consequence. There was to be no communication with anyone during those seven days – 'security, you have to understand, because of the importance of the parents' – and no cell phones or computers. They were to be as isolated as if they were on an ice floe in the Arctic Ocean. They, individually, would be picked up at the airport in Greenville, where they would turn over the cell phones. Seven days later they would be getting their cell phones back and the second half of their pay. Three hundred dollars a day was nothing to sneeze at. That was $2,100 for seven days. Tax-free because Cartwright sent them their first half in cash when she interviewed them. By phone. (If the IRS didn't know you were paid in cash, hey, why tell them?)

And every bit of communication was by snail mail.

To a Geraldine Johnson.

Through a Post Office Box in Greenville.

# CHAPTER 19

If there was any one thing Commissioner Lizzard could not do – and there were many functions he could not and an institutional laundry list of ones he could not do well – it was to be subtle. He craved attention. He was the Donald Trump of Sandersonville; overpromising and underdelivering. Every failure was someone else's doing and his machinations were p-e-r-f-e-c-t.

Subtly, however, was not his strong suit.

Worse, Lizzard's concept of cloak and dagger came from television shows and pulp fiction. In both, the writer made the difficult possible because of the power of the typewriter. Or, in the case of Lizzard's generation, the word processor. A writer can make anything workable, occasionally in the real world.

But Lizzard had not been thinking of the real world when he placed another call to Scarborough's Theatrical Emporium in Manteo. It was the only such warehouse he was aware of and was owned by a disreputable offshoot of the Scarboroughs of Buxton. Archie Scarborough junior was the son of an ancient grafter who had made his money running booze into North Carolina during Prohibition. Archie Scarborough senior became wealthy because he could read the Coast Guard manual by the book – which he had been doing for 20 years when he served in the United States Coast Guard. After he retired, he switched to the other side of the table. Archie Scarborough II, like his father, had an adjustable value system. But in his case, Scarborough II was into quasi-legal enterprises: pull tabs, bingo parlors, lottery tickets, online poker, and slot machines the police could not see.

Scarborough II was the only connection Lizzard had to the world of theater and, in this case, he, Lizzard, needed some theater. To complete the pseudo-clandestine pulp detective-inspired contrivance, the two commissioners needed three things. First, 800 pounds of gold as the hook. Second, 800 pounds of metal that looked like gold so they could fool the perpetrator of the pseudo-scam the commissioners were orchestrating. Third, and most intriguing, someone with magical skills – and Scarborough was a retired magician.

If there was any one thing Commissioner Edward Paul Lizzard III needed for this pseudo-clandestine pulp-inspired contrivance, it was a way for 800 pounds of gold to disappear into thin air.

And be replaced by 800 pounds of metal which looked like 800 pounds of gold.

# CHAPTER 20

Jerome Dawson Boone was the descendent of mudsills on both sides of his family, Dawson and Boone. While *mudsill* was not a term in wide usage in the United States west of Pitt, Greene, and Wayne counties, North Carolina, east to the Atlantic Ocean it was a common ancestry. Albeit a linguistic relic of the nation of his ancestors' births. A mudsill was the sociological term for the underclass. The term itself came from the lowest level of a house on which the entire structure sits. Mudsill, the people, were the lower class upon which the upper-class rested. Mudsills provided the labor which made the upper-class rich.

Boone's ancestors, both sides of the family, were immigrants to North Carolina by backstroke. They boarded an unworthy vessel in Bristol, England, bound for Charleston and never made it. To Charleston. The ship popped its seams and was dragged to lumber as it scattered passengers, livestock, cargo, pets, sails, and timbers along a dozen miles of the Outer Banks. Those left alive, all of them mudsills, banded together for survival. They erected a shack city from the beached timbers of the ship and intermarried for the next two centuries. They became known as BOI people, "Born on the Islands," and spent the next two centuries in the one the place in Colonial and American history that escaped a share in the "Land of Opportunity."

Boone may have come from mudsills but he was not about to end where his family had begun. BOI he fled the Outer Banks after high school and worked his way to a Bachelor's in English at Turtle College. The economy of coastal North Carolina being tight, an historical condition which will linger into the next century, he earned a teaching degree and began his career at Turtle Elementary. Third grade. By all accounts he was a good teacher. His students learned to read and write at grade level. Mathematics was problem, but then again, everyone had that problem. At the same time, he picked up extra income by serving as the business reporter for the *Turtle Gazette*, a weekly supermarket tabloid funded primarily by local real estate agents, coupon distributors and online discount services.

He hungered for better but without connections in Greenville, Wilmington, Fayetteville, or Raleigh-Durham, he was stuck in a very small town with a very small income.

What he needed was a break.

One morning he got the break he needed.

It was a call from the Commissioner of Homeland Security for Coastal North Carolina, an office and officer he had never heard of. It was all hush-hush, so to speak, but if he wanted the catbird seat, it was his. All he had to do was follow the lead of Commissioner Boris Hernandez.

"Why me?" he had asked.

"Because," Commissioner Hernandez whispered, "what's going to happen will happen in Turtle and you could be at the heart of the action and we'd like someone on the ground in Turtle. Interested?"

# CHAPTER 21

It took Noonan all of three phone calls to get a complete list of fishing rig licenses from Ocracoke to Nags Head. Even better, the list came in Excel and even Noonan knew how to alphabetize an Excel sheet. Noonan ran the names through the Sandersonville crime database, the North Carolina crime database and a handful of federal databases. What he got was exactly what he expected to find. A lot of low-level criminal infractions: DUIs, some DVs, arrests for marijuana possession, speeding, parking tickets, shoplifting, some disputes with unemployment insurance and one for clam poaching.

Clam poaching?

There were also a handful of Park Service transgressions, United States Fish and Wildlife citations and a lot of North Carolina Wildlife Commission tickets for all manner of action – or inaction: fishing without a license, overfishing, failure to catch and release, fishing out of season, fishing out of harvest area, failure to register as a fishing vessel – at a whole $33 a year! – and some pollution citations and more than a handful of tickets for overfishing. One of the tickets was for someone named Lizzard.

Well, mused Noonan, apples don't fall from the tree.

There were a few very bad boys and girls in the collection, but most of those crimes were years in the past. There were three manslaughter convictions, the most recent when Ronald Reagan was President, some burglary cases which had been dismissed in court, six armed robberies at least a decade earlier, three GTAs, all recent and all in Nags Head. (They turned out to be drunk joyriders on the beach.) There were several pending charges for serious crimes, one of them being counterfeiting. Two women were being held without bail, both, separately, for child endangerment. One man in Nags Head, a dentist, was about to go to trial for Medicaid fraud and two other men were on probation for gambling. The names of the men on probation for gambling were unquestionably Cherokee. This intrigued Noonan because gambling in North Carolina is legal on Indian Reservations – not so *off* Indian Reservations in North Carolina – so Noonan dug deeper. But he did not have to dig very deep. A few phone calls revealed the charges were for running an online operation – which was illegal in North Carolina – but the two were doing it offshore. The legal debate was four-fold: 1) How far "offshore" was their online facility and 2) How *far* offshore were they when arrested by the state authorities, 3) Did the State of North Carolina have the legal right to arrest anyone on the ocean or waterways because those were the purview of the United States Coast Guard and 4) If gambling was illegal in North Carolina except for the Indian Reservations, could someone in North Carolina who was not physically on an Indian Reservation place a bet on a computer or phone line.

The stench of politics was heady.

And Noonan was an old salt.

This salt, however, had nothing whatsoever to do with the preservation of or flavoring on food. It was a term from the ancient days when the know-how of the sailing vessels was passed on by word of mouth to the young sailors from the *old salt*, someone who had been onboard for a l-o-n-g time. In modern jargon, it translated as 'been there/done that' and the older one got, the more 'been there/done thats' there were. Noonan was sure there was a ringer in the mix. He had spent too many years dodging flying road apples.

Commissioner of the Sandersonville Homeland Security Lizzard was not the sharpest blade in the knife box but he was not a complete idiot. Even if he were, he would have had help in salting the list. *Salting the claim* was a term with which Noonan was quite familiar; his wife was Alaskan and *salting claims* was a time-honored nefarious scam. During the Alaska Gold Rush, an unscrupulous individual would load a shotgun shell with small nuggets of gold and fire them into the ground. Then prospective buyers would be *offered the opportunity* to try a few pans of earth from the claim to see how rich the diggings were. Too few nuggets meant no sale. Too many nuggets meant suspicion that the ground had been salted. Just enough was cash in the pocket for the land swindler.

Nothing had changed over the years. If you wanted someone to buy a salted argument, there had to be bait. Too much or too little was no good. Noonan knew the list he had was salted. Otherwise, he would not have been ordered to get the list in the first place. The Sandersonville Commissioner for Homeland Security would not send him on a wild goose chase unless there was a goose to follow. So, unfortunately, Noonan knew there was someone or some charge in the list of registrations that had something to do with gold that would send him off on that expected-to-be wild goose chase. It made sense

So where was the ringer, the goose that was to send him off in the Yaupon bush?

# CHAPTER 22

Rodolpho Sacerdote was not a criminal. Rather, he never considered himself a criminal. That was too low class, *déclassé* for a man of his ilk. He was an opportunist. More important, he understood the real world, not the fairy tale one of Sunday school stories, high school texts and philosophical morality tales. He was a sophisticated man who understood some basics of society. As long as the transgression you committed injured no one, no harm no foul. If you rob a bank with a gun, the authorities will search for you until pigs fly. But if you steal from the same bank with a pen, no one will admit a robbery was ever committed. That's what insurance is for: keeping your losses secret.

There was another rule he knew well: you only get one chance at big money. Done correctly and planned meticulously, you could walk away with millions.

But you were only going to get one chance to grab the brass ring.

One chance.

The game was now in play.

# CHAPTER 23

Carmella had no sense of time. She also had no sense of place. Time, a concept she could not conceive, was simply repetition. The only time, time entered her life was in the early morning sing along with numbers and colors. But even then it was rote. She had a concept of five, three, and nine but it was nebulous. As long as she had a math problem that could be solved by counting on her fingers, all was reasonably well. Colors were better as long there were not more than four and she had no comprehension of the meaning of seasons. Days of the week were meaningless labels. There was no difference between Monday and Thursday except the spelling. Saturdays and Sundays were just days she could sleep until noon. Whenever noon was.

Camilla also had no sense of distance. A ride on the school bus was neither journey nor entertainment. The scenery was meaningless to the point that if the bus window had been painted black, she would not have noticed the change. Even when she was in a moving bus, she had no sense of movement. The ride was neither short nor long. It was neither through the Sahara or a jungle. Hot and cold had no discernable meaning except when it came to food. Soft and hard, as in the bus seats, offered no distinction and the pills she took were just like food, something she swallowed. She had no taste buds or sense of smell so the concepts of bitter, sweet, pungent, spicy, sour, or bland were as foreign to her as the country of her mother's ancestors: Mexico, and that of her father, Ireland. Education was just as meaningless as the fact her mother held a Ph. D. in chemistry and her father was a federal judge.

Camilla was the perfect hostage. She had no concept of the term. She did not know what an iPhone was much less how to use it. Same with a PC. The only thing she knew for sure was the bus driver was not the regular driver. Whether he was nice or not did not register with her. She only saw him for a moment as she was being hoisted into the bus. Then her wheelchair was strapped into the bus bracing. Six kiddos later, the bus left. When the bus turned west on I-85 rather than east, it did not give her pause. It did not register she was traveling in a new direction, that the scenery was different from every other school day of the last six months. She did not know west from Adam or south from anchovies.

# CHAPTER 24

Alexander's Air Rental in Greenville had no problem renting an aircraft to Jennifer Cartwright. She was a regular customer. She always reserved the plane two weeks in advance and her checks cleared. She often came back after the rental had closed and dropped the key through the front door slot. They had never had a problem with Jennifer Cartwright. They liked her business. What was there not to like about a 60-something woman who loved to fly – and whose checks cleared?

# CHAPTER 25

When Noonan first put on his badge, there were no such forensic sciences as profiling, sociometric charting, DNA sequencing, spectral photography, or laser scaling. In most cases, it was one-and-one with suspects and your gut was the premier scientific tool. Of course, you supplanted your *gut* with the forensics of the era including ballistics, fingerprint analysis, witness statements, and good, old-fashion shoe-leather research. While technology had made convictions more inevitable – *in court* – it did nothing to supplant the human gut. Today, yesterday, a thousand years ago, a thousand years from now, the human brain was and will still be the most powerful tool in the universe.

Noonan, like every high-quality cop in America, had a highly developed sense of smell. He could smell a problem long before he discovered it. He knew there was something to find long before he actually discovered the item, evidence, weakness, or flaw.

The list of fishing rig licenses was now his hunting ground. After consolidating the list and combing duplicate addresses, he was left with 281 licenses. He reorganized the list by zip code and found that almost all of them had North Carolina addresses. There were a large number of out-of-state addresses but not any that stuck out. Three were from outside the country, two from Bermuda and one from the Bahamas. The two from Bermuda were from one company, a tourism conglomerate headquartered in Bermuda but run out of Los Angeles. He put in a call to the company for details and was told, "we'll get right on it."

"As pigs fly," Noonan said to himself when he hung up the phone.

The license out of the Bahamas looked deliciously possible but it turned out to be a subcontractor of a mega tour company whose main office in Tampa referred him to their Virginia Beach subcontractor who shunted him to the Nags Head fishing rig operation with a receptionist who knew nothing but wanted to book him on a Friday Wahoo fishing expedition because "We've just had a cancellation for a party of four. Do you have three friends? I can book you at half-price."

Then he began looking down the list for odd cities of registration in North Carolina. This turned out to be incredibly easy because the bulk of the North Carolina licenses were from cities where one would expect someone who owned a fishing rig to live: Manteo, Waves, Buxton, Pamlico City, Nags Head, Ocracoke, Avon, Hatteras, Frisco, Sandersonville, Salvo, Rodanthe and Wanchese. There were a small handful from up the beach, and a dozen reasonably close to the Outer Banks: New Bern, Washington, Morehead City, and Turtle.

Turtle?

That was odd.

Turtle wasn't coastal. It was interior and a railroad city at that.

It wasn't much of a lead but it was the best he had.

He ran his finger across the computer screen and wrote down the address – a Post Office Box – and a phone number.

A Post Office box in Turtle?

Then he saw the name of the company: AD ORO ABLE.

Nothing subtle about that. *ORO* was Italian for gold.

"OK," Noonan said to himself. "Here's my salted lead. If Homeland Security wants me to chase a wild goose, I'll chase the wild goose." He picked up the tool of Satan and evil incarnate, his cell phone, and put a call into AD ORO ABLE. No reason to use the landline to alert AD ORO ABLE he was calling from a police station. But then again, if this was the ringer, they already have his cell phone number. But then again – again – if Commissioner Lizzard wanted him to chase the wild goose, he might as well do it.

So he placed a call to AD ORO ABLE.

The woman answered the phone "Scarborough's Theatrical Emporium. How many I help you?"

Noonan, playing the cards he had been dealt, asked if this was the number for AD ORO ABLE.

"Yes, sir," she replied. "But we're in start-up mode right now. The ship is in drydock for the moment. We should be ready to troll for Red Drum in about two weeks. Can I take your name in number?"

"*Ship*," thought Noonan. "*This woman doesn't know her vocabulary. She's taking reservations for a boat, not a ship. And I'll bet you troll for wahoo but fish for red drum. Wasn't wahoo a deep-water fish while red drum were found closer to shore?*"

But to her ear he said, "Absolutely," and gave him the home phone. "Scarborough's Theatrical Emporium, That's an odd name for a fishing company. Are you located in Turtle?"

"No," the woman replied in what was clearly a canned response. "The owner has a partner in Turtle, a nephew. We're using the nephew's address. The Theatrical Emporium is actually located in Manteo. You should come by and take a look."

"Ah," Noonan said to himself, "the bait."

"I'd like to," he said to her ear. Then, to himself, "*I don't want to disappoint Sandersonville Commissioner of Homeland Security Edward Paul Lizzard III.*" Then, to the phone he said, "What's the address?"

# CHAPTER 26

When Wynter heard of the encounter he was nonplussed, in both senses of the word. He was drinking his $50^{th}$ cup of coffee for the day and set it down when Noonan handed him the address.

"Really? How convenient." His voice was flat.

"Isn't it though," Noonan replied in as flat a tone. "You'd figure they'd at least be a bit cleverer."

"Please, these are bureaucrats. They think they are being clever." Wynter shook his head. "So now we go to Manteo and nose around Scarborough's Theatrical Emporium just enough to let them know we've taken the bait."

"Sounds good to me," Noonan said as he raised the index finger of his right hand. "I will put a man on to shadow the proprietor. I don't want *anyone* to think we're not diligent in our police work."

"That is not going to make someone happy. What's that kind of scut work called on land?"

"Routine."

Wynter was silent for a moment. Then he said, "Give the man a raise."

"Better than that. The man I am going to assign, who is a woman, is on medical leave at half-pay. This puts her back at full pay."

"Aaah, but you are a clever dog," Wynter smiled mischievously.

"Not yet," Noonan replied. "See, Wynter, in my world, to quote Alaskan humorist Warren Sitka, "Moose rarely come in pairs but wolves travel in packs.""

Wynter made an odd sound and gave his head a shake. "I don't get it."

"You're not an Alaskan. All my in-laws are. Literal translation, there's more here," Noonan said as he pointed at the list of fishing rigs on the screen, "then just one lead. We've been given two clues by the brain boys. One was the AD ORO ABLE. Another something will be found somewhere in the list of FinCEN forms you brought back from D. C." He pointed at the Manilla envelope Wynter had brought back to Washington. "But my gut tells me there's more here than just two leads from two lists. Something is happening behind the scenes. There's another player involved. The brain boys didn't cook this up on their own. If I am right, they are being played by someone. We're going to have to chase wild geese but we'd better make darn sure we aren't missing something else."

"Good thought, but for the moment, we've just got your goose."

"So far. Now let's take a look at your list. There's got to be a ringer in there."

"Otherwise, I would not have been sent on the run." Wynter replied.

It took all of three minutes to find the ringer: Archie Scarborough II.

Wynter shook his head. "Subtle as a flying brick."

"How much gold did he bring in?" Noonan asked.

Wynter shuffled through the forms and found three. He handed them to Noonan. "I've got three forms from Scarborough. All just over the minimum. We're talking $36,000 in gold coins."

"Well, now we know what we're supposed to find. So the hint at gold was not a slip of the tongue. It was a deliberate hint."

"And we picked it up big time, "snapped Wynter. "And the lead to this Scarborough is the wild goose."

Noonan smiled. "Now we know what we were supposed to find. Let's see if we can discover what is really going on."

"Well, I've been over and over these forms," Wynter said as he tapped the pile on the table, "and I didn't find anything suspicious. There were only 47 forms that specifically relate to our area. Forty-three of them are for banks or precious metal operations. That leaves four."

"None of them from Turtle."

"What's with Turtle?"

There was a long silence. Finally, Noonan said. "I don't know. Just a gut feeling. The wild goose we are supposed to follow is rooted in Turtle. Why Turtle? I don't know. But I'm betting we'll be back looking at Turtle for some reason."

# CHAPTER 27

Rodolpho Sacerdote was careful to place himself at the very edge of the crowd. He wanted to be a standout but, at the same time, invisible. That, he mused to himself, was a condition for which there was no word in the English language: to be visible yet invisible at the same time. The closest term one could come up with was "unity of opposites." Physically stated, he had to be close enough to the ACTION FOR AMERICA *"FIGHT Sharia Law"* protestors dressed in pseudo-Ninja outfits to be filmed by the news crew yet, at the same time, be dressed in civilian clothing standing near enough to the anti-ACTION FOR AMERICA crowd to be considered part of that crowd. To be a standout. So he wore an orange shirt and Khakis.

He only had to stay in place long enough for the film crews to do their job.

Then he got copies of the news footage – from all three stations – and put them on CDs.

And he made sure he was wearing latex gloves for the next step of the operation.

This was his moment, when the stars aligned perfectly. Even better, he was a step back from the front tier. For the moment he would not be faceless but, at the very least, fingerprintless.

Perhaps the greatest blessing of infiltrating a radical group was it was so easy. You entered the ranks not by being a Confederate flag-waving publicity-seeking hound but by quietly showing your common sense. There were more than enough publicity hounds. Planners were rare birds. It took common sense to be a planner because that was where the money was. Rallies cost money. Club headquarters cost money. Confederate flags cost money. Placards and posters cost money. Someone had to pay for those accouterments. Publicity hounds spent money; they didn't bring it in.

Sacerdote brought in the money. It was not a lot of money. At least not at first. But it built. He was no fool. The inside men were no fools either. The FBI was there, somewhere, in the membership. Everyone knew that. No one particularly cared. No one was throwing bombs or trying to overthrow the government. Exactly the opposite. ACTION FOR AMERICA was trying to *save* America. From blacks and Jews and Muslims and gays and lesbians.

ACTION FOR AMERICA was typical of far-right-wing groups. They were actually two separate operations under the same philosophical umbrella. The largest contingent were the publicity hounds. These were the highly visible, slogan-mouthing wing nuts who appeared on television. They were not particularly bright when it came to a philosophy beyond what they had been told to say. But then again, one did need a Ph. D. to talk about the danger of Sharia law. You did not even have to know what Sharia law was to be against it. All you had to do was talk about Sharia law being like a growing cancer – don't use the word metastasizing because that was a 12-dollar word.

All these folks had to be scary. Real scary! The kind of people mom and dad would see on news programs and pray their children never dressed up in pseudo-Ninja outfits, militia uniforms, Confederate flag jackets, white robes, or caps with swastikas. These publicity hounds had to be just scary enough the smaller, inner circle of the organization could go to the money people and say conflicting things at the same time: give us money to keep our wackos in check and, at the same time, to give us enough money to keep our wackos on the street to scare the public into voting Republican.

Sacerdote was a gift of the gods to ACTION FOR AMERICA. He came with money. That for sure meant he was not FBI. The FBI did not come with money. They slithered in at the bottom of the organization and tried to worm their way up the internal food chain. If you came with money, you went right to the top of the internal food chain.

And you could call a lot of shots.

Even better than that, Sacerdote came with money that was untraceable. That is to say, he did not come with cash. He came with gold. This was a god-send to the publicity hounds because there was no fear that the money, as in cash, they had received could be traced. Give a publicity hound a thousand dollars in cash and every one of the $100 bills had a serial number and the FBI could track every one of the bills. But when it came to gold, the publicity hounds were in the clear. Their expenses were paid to come to the rallies. Their hotel and food were paid during the rallies. When they left, each was given a gold coin. Depending on the price of gold, that was about $1,300 a Troy ounce. It was something they could put in their pocket, hide in their shoe or even swallow if they believed their own conspiracy theories about the United States government. When they got home in Philadelphia, Atlanta, Detroit, or Grand Junction, they simply exchanged the gold coin for cash.

Gold coins could not be traced back to a source.

Rodolpho Sacerdote brought gold coins to ACTION FOR AMERICA.

Since he came with the money, he was in the inner circle.

Where he had access to all of the records.

On the computers he bought for ACTION FOR AMERICA.

Backed up every night.

This made it very easy for Sacerdote to implant the seed of a radical conspiracy.

Was it a beaut!

His biggest problem was not coming up with a conspiracy; it was inventing an unbelievable yet believable campaign of terror. It had to be *just credible enough* to attract the attention of the Office of Homeland Security but *not so incredible* as to be written off as a right-wing delusion. It was a delicate ballet of fantasy versus reality. He solved the problem in a unique manner. Rather than developing a rock-solid plan of action, he suggested a laundry list of activities which could be perpetrated on coastal North Carolina dependent on how much money came in. Key to the conspiracy, it would be centered on the purchase and surreptitious placing of packages of triacetone triperoxide, TATP, a white crystalline explosive powder, in a spectrum of locations, including telephone exchange centers, courthouses, bridges, and water utility conduits. There were also suggestions of sending small packages of TATP through the mail to judges, mayors, and county supervisors from Virginia Beach to Ocracoke and as far inland as Greenville, Goldsboro, and New Bern. At the same time, assorted members of ACTION FOR AMERICA would plant, mail, graffiti-write radical slogans in the area. Then, secondarily, after the packages had delivered their deadly load, ACTION FOR AMERICA rallies would be held in the same areas demanding the expulsion of all Muslims from the United States, a permanent ban on Muslims coming into the United States, the destruction of all mosques in the United States and heightened security

The extent of the terror campaign was only limited by the amount of money available for the venture. The more money, the more destruction there was going to be. For $15 million, in gold, ACTION FOR AMERICA could deliver the whole enchilada.

According to the flash drives Sacerdote gave to his childhood connection in Manteo.

Who passed the information along to the Department of Homeland Security in North Carolina.

Who suggested Homeland Security could catch the perpetrators *in flagrante delicto.*

All that was needed was 800 pounds of gold as bait. Cleverly done, with a bit of prestidigitation, fake gold could be substituted for real gold.

And Homeland Security would come up with a coup – and a lot of publicity – without a dime of United States money spent in the process.

Was Homeland Security interested?

# CHAPTER 28

Noonan and Wynter were working on their third cup of morning coffee, trying to make sense of the gold standard. Historically they both knew at one time the United States dollar was based on gold. This was the reason it was called the gold standard. At that time, whenever it was, an American dollar was backed up by a dollar's worth of gold in the national treasury. It was a lot more complicated than that, of course, because you could go into a bank and get $100 in either paper money or gold.

But when had that changed and why? Even more important, what did it mean for using gold at that moment?

Finding the history of the gold standard was as easy as spelling Wikipedia. Basically, and historically, gold has been the chosen medium of exchange since the dawn of time. With Western Civilization, with the exception of Africa where gold was so common it had no real value. Gold was prized as a valuable metal because the element had a very low melting point compared to other metals. This meant the gold could be formed into jewelry or used to fill teeth if it was not used as money. The United States went on the gold standard in 1879 and the standard was a dollar of gold in the possession of the United States government for every United States paper dollar printed. When you went into a bank to withdraw money, you could get either gold or paper dollars.

This practice came to a screeching halt in 1933 when America fell into the Great Depression. Since gold kept its value while paper dollars fluctuated in worth, people closed their accounts in banks and took their savings in gold. They hid the gold, called hoarding, which reduced the amount of gold in banks. Depositors did not want paper dollars, only gold. Since the banks had no gold, they went under. The situation was so bad FDR declared a Bank Holiday – from March 6 to March 13, 1933 – shortly after taking office.

To stimulate the economy, FDR needed money to circulate. But money was not circulating because people were hoarding their gold anticipating the economy was not going to get better any time soon. But FDR thus needed to get the gold back into the banks to stabilize the economy. At the same time, he needed more money, as in cash, to stimulate the economy. But the government could not just print money. Because the American dollar was tied to the gold standard, the government needed a dollar in gold to come into the treasury for every dollar it printed on paper.

This was not going to happen so FDR and Congress cleverly did two things at the same time. First, they outlawed the use of gold in banks. And they outlawed the ownership of gold by Americans. All gold taken in by banks had to be sold to the United States government at a set price. This pulled gold out of circulation for day-to-day activities. Now people *had* to use paper money.

The next part was tricky. The United States government had to increase the supply of money, as in cash, in the economy without inflating the value of each dollar. If the United States remained on the gold standard, printing more paper money would have reduced the value of each paper dollar printed. In other words, if the United States government had $1 billion in gold it could have $1 billion in paper money in circulation. But if the United States government printed another $1 billion in paper money without another $1 billion in gold in the treasury, every paper dollar in circulation would be worth half its printed value. Printing more money would not stimulate more economic activity. It would just cause merchants to raise their prices.

So FDR and Congress went one better. They pulled America off the gold standard and had the value of every dollar based on the *overall health* of the American economy. It worked and it would not be until the 1970s that Americans could own gold again.

Gold never regained its preeminent status in the United States. There was a small contingent of what were known as 'gold bugs" who hoarded gold 'just in case' the America economy tumbled, but other than those individuals, most Americans only had gold in jewelry or their teeth.

But when it came to criminal activity, gold had a distinct advantage: it was untraceable. In whatever form it was, there was no provenance. If you had a bar of gold, no one asked where you got it. And there was no way to trace its ancestry. The only thing you had to do was declare the sale of gold as income. You did not mess with the IRS.

On the other hand, gold was unbelievably difficult to move. A million dollars in gold was about 60 pounds. A strong man could pick up 60 pounds but he would need a car or a truck to make his getaway. The larger the amount of gold demanded, the heavier the loot was.

All of this was generally known to both Noonan and Wynter but did not give them a clue as to what game the two commissioners of the Department of Homeland Security were playing.

Wynter sighed. "Following this Scarborough fellow has been a real bore. He isn't doing anything I can see that's suspicious."

"That might be the point," Noonan said. "We're supposed to be bored watching him. The commissioners are frying other fish right now."

"A nice Outer Banks expression," Wynter shook his head. "What should we be doing?"

"Well, I'd say we follow the money. That's an old law and order expression, by the way."

"That I know," Wynter said humorously. "I've watched LAW AND ORDER. So, how exactly should we be following the money?" He paused. "And which money should we be following?"

"By the process of elimination. We know, or at least assume, the commissioners are dealing with gold in some capacity. So, who deals in gold?"

Wynter had an answer. "Precious metal people, jewelers, dentists." Well, let's ask around.

Noonan chuckled. "You Navy guys! Subtle. We need to be subtle. Realistically, whatever the commissioners are doing involves gold. We know it's not coming in from outside the country because none of the FinCEN forms indicate large amounts of gold to individuals or small businesses. So the gold has to be being collected from inside the country. It's doubtful the gold is coming from Fort Knox so it has to be accumulated here. Probably in the coastal North Carolina area. I don't see the commissioners including any more commissioners on this caper. This is a publicity stunt."

"And they want the glory for themselves," Wynter cut it. "I understand that."

"I agree," Noonan nodded his head. "So the gold is local. Large amounts will have to come from precious metal dealers. How many are we talking about?"

Wynter was on his tool of Satan as Noonan continued to speak.

Noonan continued to talk while Wynter kept tapping his phone. "We should not be talking to the precious metal people just yet. We don't want them knowing we are onto their scheme. Let's see if we can find out which dealer is holding back for a big sale."

"How do we do that?" Wynter asked and then added, "There are 16 businesses listed as precious metal dealers in coastal North Carolina."

"Let me guess, none in Turtle?"

"Correct. None in Turtle. There are 16 but it depends on what you call coastal North Carolina. There are two in Greenville, for instance. Is that coastal North Carolina?"

"I'd say no. My guess, and it's just a guess, the commissioners want to be close to the source of the gold. There isn't a precious metal dealer in Sandersonville and I'll bet the nearest one to Sandersonville would be in Manteo. All of the hamlets on the Outer Banks are pretty small."

"None in Avon. One in Elizabeth City and one in Manteo."

"Manteo," Noonan smiled. "Of course. Boris Hernandez is based out of Manteo. I'll bet that's our boy."

"And our wild goose is out of Manteo as well."

"Good, good!" Noonan was excited. "Our research is paying off!"

"So we pay them a visit?" Wynter started to rise.

"No, no." Noonan put his hand on Wynter left forearm. "Subtly is the name of the game. We don't want anyone to know we've solved the riddle."

"Well, OK. So, how do we go about this *subtly?*" Wynter accented the word *subtly* with derision.

"We find a stalking horse. Do you know what a stalking horse is?"

Wynter was silent for a moment. "OK, I'll bite."

"In the old days, hunters in Europe went after deer using a horse. But they didn't ride the horse, they hid behind it. They would guide the horse near enough to the deer to get a shot. From the point of view of the deer, the horse was not a danger. It's just another four-legged animal."

"So we need a stalking horse."

"We need a stalking horse."

"Do you have one in mind?"

"As a matter of fact," Noonan said smiling. "I do."

# CHAPTER 29

Archie Scarborough was a saint. Not a Saint as in Saint Peter or Saint Christopher, usually referred to as St. Peter and St. Christopher – but THE SAINT. Roger Moore as THE SAINT. If you were too young to remember THE SAINT, think LIVE AND LET DIE or A VIEW TO A KILL. THE SAINT, a television program which ran on British television from 1962 to 1969 – and in more than 60 countries to this day since then, starring Roger Moore as Simon Templar. Templar was a rogue whose clients could not use the police or courts to 'resolve their issues.' Templar used his talents, some of them beyond the bounds of the law, to 'resolve' those issues. He never went 'bad.' That is, he never went 'bad' if you were the person who retained his service. On the flip side of the coin, it was quite another matter.

[As a matter of entertainment fact, had Noonan's father been asked of THE SAINT, he, the father, would have scoffed at Roger Moore as Simon Templar. He, again, the father, would have pointed to the actor who personified British upper-class villains, George Sanders. Sanders was Simon Templar in five British films in the 1930s. Interestingly, and oddly, THE SAINT, a *British* upper-class rogue, was penned by a *Chinese* author, Leslie Charteris Bower-Yin. Bower-Yin moved to Los Angeles in the 1930s to work in the movie industry for Paramount Pictures. He changed his name to Leslie Charteris. But he could not change his nationality and, because of the Chinese Exclusion Act, had to continually renew his temporary visitor's visa every six months. Until 1943, when Congress granted Charteris and his daughter the right to permanent residency, five years before Noonan, the son, was born.]

"I just want to make it clear," THE SAINT Scarborough said as he sat down with Lizzard and Hernandez, "you came to me. I'm helping you but I am not in the driver's seat."

"Fine, fine, fine," Hernandez so quickly it was as though he was completing Scarborough's sentence. "If we had time to speak of the niceties, well, we would." He smiled. "But we don't. From the information we have, what you provided from your source, and what we know this, this, this. . ."

" . . . matter," Lizzard cut in. "This matter is of national importance. We have it from the highest authority within Homeland Security that we should take this *matter*," he glanced at Hernandez as he put emphasis on the word *matter*, "seriously. We do not have a lot of time as things are moving quickly."

"Fine," Scarborough said with a straight face. "Let me tell you what I recommend. We, you, are talking a lot of money. Gold, actually. The ground rules are pretty solid. You want the ACTION FOR AMERICA conspirator to see the gold and test the gold. Then you want the gold switched out so the ACTION FOR AMERICA conspirator runs away with fake gold thinking it is real gold."

"In a nutshell," Hernandez said smiling, "yeah."

"As long as we are clear that I am not involved further in this, this, *matter*." He stressed the word *matter* as he thumped his chest for emphasis. "I've set the stage, so to speak, but from here on out, it's your ballgame. If things go wrong, I'm not involved."

"Your plan seems foolproof, Archie," Lizzard liked being friendly. "It's a good plan and should work. We'll have some police to watch the real gold just to make sure no one gets sticky fingers."

"Fine, fine." Scarborough said. "I've made all the arrangements in Turtle and we'll go over them in a moment, but, for the moment, there are two things I need to put on the table."

"I thought all the details had been worked out?" Hernandez was annoyed. "What's to talk about?"

"Nothing to do with the switch, if that's what you are asking. Just two things for you to keep in mind. First, when the . . ." he stalled.

" . . . matter," said Hernandez.

". . . matter," continued Scarborough, "is wrapped up there could be a legal problem. What the ACTION FOR AMERICA conspirator is actually absconding with is fake gold. He's not going to get 800 pounds of authentic gold. He's going to get 800 pounds of metal painted gold. Lead. Lead's selling for under a dollar a pound on the market. Which means the ACTION FOR AMERICA conspirator is getting under $1,000. A good lawyer would get him off on a misdemeanor."

"Oh, we're not worried about what happens to the perpetrators," Lizzard began and then corrected himself. "That is to say, we're not worried about the end game. We just need to nip this conspiracy in the bud. Once we get the conspirators we'll let the Department of Justice the actual legal work."

"So the Department of Justice has seen the material from ACTION FOR AMERICA? It has an opinion?"

Hernandez was suddenly skittish. "We passed the material up the Homeland Security chain of command. It's above our pay grade to act on our own. We were told to gather more information, documents, and nip any covert action in the bud. The legal end of this matter is with the legal beagles, er, eagles in the department."

"OK," Scarborough said as he patted his chest. "Just so that base is covered. Second, and just as important, the real gold must be paid for before this, this . . ."

". . . matter," everyone said in unison.

"matter," Scarborough continued. "starts. Keep in mind that the gold, the actual metal, is going to be part of the legal case. Legally, and I am no lawyer, legally, I suspect, you cannot say that ACTION FOR AMERICA stole 800 pounds of gold for a nefarious plot without having the 800 pounds of actual gold. No jury will believe someone is stupid enough to get 800 pounds of painted lead thinking it is gold. The jury is going to want to know there **really was** 800 pounds of gold involved and that specific gold, every ounce of it, was owned by the United States government. If the gold was not actually owned by the United States government, and I mean with authentic paperwork, it is going to look like an elaborate prank on the United States government. Then we are all going to look very stupid. I don't want to look stupid. It's bad for business."

Hernandez shook his head. "Archie," he got personal. "Homeland Security has purchased the gold. We have assured the powers that be the gold is not at risk. They, that is, the powers that be, have approved the plot. The actual gold is only needed for the approval of the ACTION FOR AMERICA conspirator. Then the switch will be made. Homeland Security will have guards – along with the Sandersonville police, let me quickly add – who will keep an eye on the actual gold. Once the ACTION FOR AMERICA conspirator is downwind, the gold will be returned by armored car to a secure location."

Scarborough started to issue a cautionary note but Hernandez cut him off. "And, and, and, just in case things get messed up at the warehouse, we have a perimeter plan. Even if someone can get the gold out of the warehouse they will not be able to use any road or any river to move the gold. The State Troopers will be on alert as will the Navy and Coast Guard. That gold is not going anywhere."

"OK. Sounds good to me." Scarborough thumped his chest again. "I just want to make it clear I am not on the operational end of this matter. I just came up with the idea and you approved the idea. I'm the nuts-and-bolts person."

Hernandez cut him off. "Yes, yes, yes. We all know that. Homeland Security is in charge of the operation and we appreciate your efforts. The gold will be under our protection. Every step of the way. You've done your job. We appreciate you coming here today. From here on out, we'll run the operation."

Scarborough smiled and thumped his chest yet again. He rose, shook the hands of the commissioners and left their office.

"Jumpy, isn't he," Hernandez said after Scarborough held left the room.

"No reason for him to be," Lizzard replied. "Everything is under control. We don't have a thing in the world to worry about. We are going to look so good in the press and our grandparents will rise out of their graves and give us a cheer."

"In two days," Lizzard added with a smile.

"Yup. Forty-eight hours and counting."

# CHAPTER 30

S acerdote spent two hours in Kitty Hawk filling out paperwork and paying the admission and landing strip fees. He received the badges and exhibitor gate pass. Before he left the grounds he locked his plane wings to the tie-downs in his space adjacent to the landing strip. He was pleased to see the beehive of activity for the celebration of the Wright Brothers flight. Never in their wildest imagination could the Wright Brothers have anticipated what was going to happen this long after they made the first controlled flight of a heavier-than-air aircraft. Well, history was going to be made here again.

In about 24 hours.

Give or take.

# CHAPTER 31

"Chelsea! Heinz Noonan here!" His voice was loud and clear. Wynter gave Noonan a strange look. Then, silently, he whispered to himself, "Chelsea?"

Noonan ignored him. The phone was on speaker so Wynter did not raise his voice.

"Captain Noonan!" Chelsea said excitedly. "Missing another dematerializing armored car?" Her voice was mocking. "And *you are* calling the Pamlico City Police Department for help. Again. Right?"

"Heinz, Chelsea! Heinz! It's only *captain* when we're on a caper! How are you feeling?"

"Fine, Heinz." There was hesitancy in her voice.

"No, actually you feel very sick right now."

"Really?"

"Absolutely. Terribly ill. In fact, you feel so bad you need to take the rest of the day off."

There was a long pause. Then she got the message. "Oh, yes. Certainly. I'm so sick. Terrible to happen in the middle of the day. And I'm to go home . . ." she did not complete the sentence.

"Absolutely. Shower and dress well. See, you are planning on getting married, and you will be visiting jewelry stores looking for a ring with your fiancé."

"My fiancé, how nice. Do I know him?"

Noonan gave Wynter a nod of his head. "Not yet. His name is Wynter Morales. He's a Navy man. You'll love him. You want to marry him. You want a special ring with lots of gold."

91

"No diamonds?"

"Diamonds are fine. Gold is what you are going to be asking about."

"Ahhh, undercover. Does the Pamlico City Police Department know about this work?"

"Not yet. But they will. You're the best, Chelsea. Give me your home address and Wynter will pick you up there."

"Is he going to be dressed in a uniform?"

Noonan looked at Wynter and asked. "You going to be dressed in a uniform?"

"Should I be?" Wynter asked with a look of helplessness on his face.

"With your haircut, yeah." Noonan replied. Then to Chelsea, "Yes, he will be wearing a uniform. Be nice to our servicemen."

Chelsea gave him an address. Noonan gave the address to Wynter. He hung up the phone and said to Wynter, "Give her an hour."

"Who is she?"

Noonan smiled. "A very bright law enforcement officer. She was a crackerjack on one of my cases, the Matter of the Dematerializing Armored car. Ask her about it. It will be a great conversation starter."

# CHAPTER 32

Historically, the first gold rush in American history was not in California. It was in North Carolina. In 1799, half a century ahead of California and an entire century ahead of Alaska. In that year, the son of a former Hessian soldier, Conrad Reed, found a shiny yellow rock on his family farm in Cabarrus County. The rock weighed about 16 pounds. His father used the stone as a doorstop for three years. When he went to sell the stone, it was worth $3,600 – in an era when $3.50 was a week's wages. When the father discovered the true value of the shiny rock, he began a mining operation and died a wealthy man. In 1845. Three years before the California Gold Rush. The Reed Mine operated until 1912 and produced so much gold a mint had to be built in Charlotte to handle the mine's output.

More than a century later and 350 miles to the west, there was going to be another gold strike.

It was hard to be faceless in Turtle. Small towns are notorious for everyone knowing everyone else's business. But Sacerdote had to stay faceless.

Sacerdote wormed his way in the pickup truck around the outskirts of Turtle, which, considering its size, was not difficult. Perhaps the great blessing of Turtle was the vast network of abandoned tracks, truncated spur lines, and pullouts where slow trains could have pulled off the mainline to let faster trains speed by. Bouncing over sets of tracks overgrown with weeds and swamp grass, he made his way to a ramshackle structure alongside a spur line to a spur line to a spur line. The shack sat in the shade of a copse of trees. Some rusting farm equipment was beside the shack and a collapsing barn were the only structures on the property.

Sacerdote parked his pickup, the perfect undercover vehicle for a community like Turtle, walked to the door of the shack and pushed his way inside.

The outside of the shed was a clue as to its interior condition. Inside the structure was a single large room, twice the size of a standard garage. The roof was sagging from age and the single window in the structure had a spider web of breaks. In the center of the doublewide area were two battered wheelbarrows. Only one was needed but with so much at stake, a backup was a good idea.

But he wasn't here for the wheelbarrows. He was here to make sure no homeless person had moved in. At least not for the next 36 hours. After that, anyone could live here.

The shed was empty.

No unwanted residents here.

Sacerdote smiled.

# CHAPTER 33

Jerome Dawson Boone got the call forwarded from *Turtle Gazette*; the first time any call had been forwarded to any reporter for the *Turtle Gazette*. In fact, the *Turtle Gazette* did not get any calls for news coverage. Coupons, yes. Advertising, yes. PTA, Community Council – in the singular – and State Senate and House hearings, yes. But news, NOPE; all in caps.

Boone took the call with as professional a voice as he could muster.

"Commissioner Lizzard? What a pleasure. What can I do for the security of the United States?"

Lizzard preened at the other end of the line.

"Mr. Boone. Yes, there is something you can do for the security of the United States. We are expecting some activity in the Turtle area very soon. Will you make yourself available?"

*Available!? Absolutely he would be available!*

"Yes, sir. Is there a set time for this, this, event?"

"We refer to it as a matter. There will be a general time of activity in the sense we will know ahead of time when the matter will come to a head. We will give you a few hours' heads-up, so to speak. We anticipate there will be a need for a photographer and a news camera person. Do you know such individuals?"

*Share this glory of the moment with anyone else?! Hardly!*

"I can handle the photography, sir. And I have an arrangement with a local station for footage. I can take the footage you need, we need, with my cell phone."

"Fine, fine. Keep in mind this is all very hush-hush. We don't want the word to leak that something is happening in the Turtle area. I am counting on your discretion."

"I am trustworthy, sir. My lips are sealed."

"A good way to have them in matters such as this. Now, I need your cell phone number. I promise I will not call in the middle of the night but when things start to happen, you know, I want to make sure you are in the loop."

Boone gave Lizzard his cell phone number and then asked, "How much advance warning will I get? I mean, I have to make sure I have everything you need in my care. Will this assignment last an hour, day, you know, I'd like to do some advance planning."

There was silence on the phone for a while. Then Lizzard added quietly, "This is all very hush-hush now so don't tell anyone. Not a wife. . "

"I don't have one."

". . .or a girlfriend, parent, minister. No one."

"No one."

"The matter will last a full day starting as early as three a.m. In Manteo. Then there will be a press conference a few days later. The matter will take place in Turtle and the press conference in Manteo. Well, I'll, make sure you are front and center for the press conference."

"Well, I appreciate that, sir."

"Good, good. I'll give you a few hours' notice. But you talk to no one, hear. No one."

"Yes, sir."

"Hush-hush. This matter is all hush-hush. You will start in Manteo at about three a.m. so be prepared for a long day."

# CHAPTER 34

If Noonan expected Wynter and Chelsea to take a few days to do the undercover work, he was in for a surprise. Wynter picked up Chelsea at her apartment at noon and by 4 p.m., they were back in Noonan's office. That took the 'Bearded Holmes' by surprise.

"I hate to ask. Was it a bust?"

Chelsea gave him a you've-got-to-kidding-me-with-a-line-like-that look. "No," she said a bit irritated. "We're back with a triple."

"Triple?" Noonan was confused.

"We hit three home runs," Wynter cut in. He put an arm affectionally around Chelsea's shoulders. "The loving couple hit three homeruns."

"Which one do you want first," Chelsea asked excitedly.

Noonan sank into his desk chair and gave kind of a circular motion with his right hand to indicate they should tell all.

"You go first," Wynter pointed at Chelsea.

"Frankly, Captain."

"Heinz."

"Right, Heinz. Frankly, it was quite easy. We started in Manteo because that was where the action was."

"Action?" Noonan had a puzzled look on his face.

"Well," Wynter cut in, "we, Chelsea and I, decided to start in Manteo rather than work our way up the coast. It's the largest city on the coast, is headquarters for Boris Hernandez and has Scarborough's Theatrical Emporium." Noonan gave Wynter a strange look and Wynter filled him in on, "Scarborough's Theatrical Emporium, the owner of the AD ORO ABLE fishing rig."

"Right," said Noonan now that his mind was refreshed.

"It was actually pretty easy," Chelsea said excitedly. "We went to three jewelry stores and they all told us the same thing. There has been a shortage of gold."

"Local gold," Wynter cut it. "Local gold. All the jewelers said the local gold came from a local company, Patterson Precious Metals. In Manteo."

"We were cool as cucumbers," Chelsea said as she smiled. "The jewelers were so nice. They told us all about the gold business and how Patterson was the local supply point. Patterson bought old jewelry, nuggets, and ingots, then melted them all together. The melted gold went to a local refinery and then to local jewelers. Local jewelers like to buy local gold, a chamber of commerce kind of thing."

"So we asked who the local refinery was," Wynter cut it. "Guess who it was."

"Patterson," Noonan said.

"Yup," Chelsea said excitedly. "I played the dumb blonde and asked when the local gold was going to be available."

"Let me guess," Noonan said. "Soon."

"Correct!" Chelsea was excited. "'Oh, the refinery is local?' I asked and the jeweler said 'yes.' Do you want a tour?'"

"And you said, 'yes,' of course." Noonan was smiling.

Chelsea smiled. "Absolutely. So the jeweler made a call. I got a personal tour of Patterson Precious Metals in Manteo. You would never guess what is just sitting in a large pile in the back of their vault."

"Gold," said Noonan.

"Bingo," said Chelsea. "I asked what it was and the nice tour man said it was 800 pounds for a special client. That was why there had been a local shortage."

"Bet he didn't say who," Noonan said.

"Wrong!" Chelsea was giddy with excitement. "Sometimes it pays to be a dumb blonde."

"And she's not even blonde," Wynter cut in.

"Forget the blonde," Noonan said. "Patterson's actually **told** you who the client was?"

"Yup. The United States government. That's what the tour man said. The United States government."

Noonan shook his head. Then he looked at Chelsea. "You did very well, very well. One very interesting piece of the puzzle has just fallen into place."

"But wait," Wynter said mimicking the late-night advertisements. "There's more! While she was playing the dumb blonde, I went over to Scarborough's Theatrical Emporium. I didn't see your police person so she must be very good at her job."

"Maybe too good," Noonan said. "I'll tell her to be a bit more visible. Did you actually go inside Scarborough's Theatrical Emporium?"

"Yup. It was a strange building. It was big on the outside and little on the inside. Too little on the inside for just storage back there."

Noonan gave a kind of knowing grunt.

"I kind of looked over the stock and was going to ask something stupid when this Mexican came in with the shortest, baldest man I had ever seen."

"Hernandez and Lizzard!" Noonan was excited. "You actually saw them?"

"The little guy I didn't know but I recognized the voice of the Mexican. They were not in Scarborough's very long. Apparently, they wanted to talk with the owner, Archie Scarborough, but he was out. So they just left a message. Something like, 'Is everything ready to go?' The woman at the counter said she didn't know but she'd ask."

"That's all? 'Is everything ready to go?'" Noonan was still smiling.

"That's what she said. They left and I followed them out."

A look of horror crossed Noonan's face. Wynter put him at ease quickly.

"They didn't see me, couldn't see me. I was a block back across the street and there were crowds on the street. They only walked about six blocks and went in the back door of a post office. I guess that's where Homeland Security is located for coastal North Carolina."

"Probably," said Noonan. "But we're just nipping around the edges of what's going on. Whatever it is our *friends* in Homeland Security are going involves 800 pounds of gold and it is going to happen fairly quickly."

"Well, whatever it is," Chelsea added, "if Homeland Security is involved it's going to be a complete disaster. I hope I'm still sick tomorrow?" She looked at Noonan and Wynter pensively.

# CHAPTER 35

There was nothing unusual about the bus. Not that Camilla would have noticed anything unusual about the bus even if there had been something unusual to notice.

This bus.

Or Any bus.

Camilla was incapable of conventional, fourth-grade thoughts. She was not of the fourth grade. She was of the ozone if you asked other fourth graders. Her parents knew her as a "special needs" student. The Turtle Elementary School knew her as a "special education" student and the State of North Carolina Department of Education knew her as someone under the age of 18 who was required by law to be given an education.

Camilla did not have the capacity to understand her special needs. Nor did it register she was with similarly afflicted fourth grade students. She did not even notice the four other kiddos on the bus, kiddos being the operative word for "special needs" or "special education" students. She didn't know autism from blindness or Downs Syndrome from TBI. She had no friends on this bus. They were just globs of protoplasm who were loaded with her. One at a time they were loaded onto the bus. One at a time they were offloaded along the route to where she was off-loaded to a place – in her mind, just a place, not a specific geographical location – where she was fed, bathed and put to bed and then, on most mornings, roused to go to school on the same bus with the same kiddos she did not recognize every morning just as she did not recognize them every afternoon.

When loaded, the bus took off.

Heading toward Greenville.

The opposite direction from Manteo.

Camilla did not notice because she did not know east from Adam or south from anchovies.

# CHAPTER 36

When the 800 pounds of gold was collected – and paid for – and the check cleared – Michael Patterson called the North Carolina Coastal Commissioner of Homeland Security and reported the gold as ready to travel. Boris Hernandez said something along the lines of "well done" or "good job" and made the arrangements for the pickup the next morning.

Saturday.

At 3 a.m.

"Three a.m.?"

"Correct. We will not need your assistance. We will have our own labor force, so to speak," Hernandez told him. "We just need you on hand to sign the gold out. Transfer the gold, that is. To the Office of Homeland Security."

"You're the boss," Patterson said as he looked over the account. All had been paid in full. He had done his job. And he did not even have to hire an armored car to make the delivery. Sweet.

# CHAPTER 37

Noonan got the call from his majesty Edward Paul Lizzard III Friday morning.

On the electronic tool of Satan.

Noonan was to be with Wynter no later than 11 a.m. that morning for a phone call from the Homeland Security Task Force for Coastal North Carolina which was then meeting in the backroom of the Sandersonville Surf Fisherman Club. To which Noonan had two questions: "What was the Joint Homeland Security Task Force for Coastal North Carolina" and "Why meet in the back room of the Sandersonville Surf Fisherman's Club instead of the Sandersonville Police Department Command room?"

To the first, Lizzard replied that it was a recently-formed venture and Noonan would be under its command in Turtle. As to the second, this was all "hush-hush, you know, Captain. We don't want the bad boys and girls to know we know who they are."

The twin explanations made no sense but one cannot argue with those up the administrative food chain.

# CHAPTER 38

I t was the kind of a gig he liked. Big bucks upfront, smaller amounts at the back end. All he had to do was about two hours' worth of work. He came in from Arizona, off the desert. For a friend from Vietnam. And Africa. And Syria. Fellow soldier. Fellow merc. With cash. The best kind of friends to have. Friend, actually. And for a caper like this, you only wanted one. Friend and caper.

He had been letting his hair and beard grow for six months. Was going to wear a girdle to add 50 pounds to his 160-pound frame. Got some ratty clothes from the homeless shelter and a ripped leather jacket two sizes too large to make him look like a biker. Motorcycle, not the high desert bike he used to get groceries.

He had to make it look good. Gloves, a bottle of vinegar, tuning fork. Just enough to look good. Only the boots had to be first class. He would not have to walk that far but he would have to walk fast. Then drive slowly. For hours.

# CHAPTER 39

The nondescript bus painted school bus yellow-orange made the outskirts of Greenville just about the same time that the first call came into the Turtle Elementary School main office. The Special Education bus had not made its first stop. Mrs. Tomanak had been at the bus stop for half an hour and Jerome still had not arrived. Mrs. Tomanak wanted to know when the bus from Turtle was going to arrive. Had it left on time? Yes, the principal told her, the bus had left on time. As a matter of fact, she had been outside the school when it was loaded with the six kiddos.

The principal called Rampart Transportation. Rampart Transportation punched the GPS for the bus and it came back as being located in the parking garage. But the bus was not in the parking garage. Rampart placed a cell phone call to the driver and he was wahoo fishing off the Hatteras coast. He said he had been given the day off – with pay – by someone who had called from the main office in Rampart in Charlotte.

So he had taken the day off.

With pay.

Was there a problem?

A search of the garage led to the discovery of the GPS for Rampart Bus 348 in the chassis of Rampart Bus 356, a bus under repair. That was when the North Carolina State Troopers were called. The search started well east of where the bus should have made its last stop, at the confluence of the Alligator River and the Albemarle Sound, and then proceeded west. Backroads, turnouts and abandoned roadways were searched.

When no bus was found, the search extended from Turtle west toward Greenville.

But by then Rampart Transportation Bus 348 was locked in the warehouse of a soil dispensing operation at the north end of Greenville.

And the kiddos were in a large, carpeted room complete with plastic dinosaur toys, stuffed animals, swinging chairs, and gameboards, a replica of the special education room at Turtle Elementary School.

And Turtle School Nurse Jennifer Cartwright had secured all of the medications the six kiddos would need for the next three days. Four at the most. But more likely two.

Or even one.

Then the kiddos would go home.

And no one in Greenville had seen Jennifer Cartwright. She was just a voice on the phone and, since the money was good, no one had asked to see her. It had all been an arm's length transaction.

# CHAPTER 40

Noonan and Wynter were mentally maneuvering humanoid figures over an imaginary multi-dimensional chessboard when a call from Navy headquarters came in for Wynter. They were sitting with Chelsea in the back booth of the Sandersonville Grille, waiting for the 11 a.m. hush-hush phone call. Noonan was supposedly on special assignment so he should not have been at the Sandersonville Police Station.

So he wasn't.

The call to Wynter was not directly from Naval headquarters in Washington D. C. It was indirect. Through the Judge Advocate General in North Carolina. It was still down the chain of command. Wynter was just told he had been assigned to work with the Sandersonville Office of Homeland Security. He had another cup of coffee. Noonan settled for sparkling water. Chelsea opted for a burger.

"At the present time, I have been reassigned," Wynter said when he punched the cell phone off. He smiled and continued, "to work with Homeland Security and my contact is you." He pointed at Noonan with his cell phone. "That makes it official. We are a team."

"Yeah," said Noonan. "Frankly, I didn't even know there was a JAG office in North Carolina,"

"That makes two of us," retorted Wynter. "But that's the Navy for you."

"Where does that leave me?" snapped Chelsea. "I'm not in the Navy or the Sandersonville Police Department."

"You're sick," Noonan told her looking over the top of his glasses. "Terribly sick. At least for a day or two. And you're helping Uncle Heinz and you know how those old codgers are! Cranky and hard to deal with!"

"That appears to be the requirement for command in North Carolina," she snapped.

"Now that we're all on the same page, so to speak," Noonan said. "Let's go over what we have, what we think we have and what we guess is going to happen."

"We've got zip," Chelsea snarled. "We know that Homeland Security is doing something with 800 pounds of gold within the next two days. It has some connection to Turtle, Manteo and Archie Scarborough."

"And whatever it is, it is a very bad idea," Wynter shook his head. "It's hard for me to believe that Homeland Security could come up with a *good* idea. Worse, any idea it comes up with is going to be without a backstop. It will have no Plan B."

"I have to agree with both of you," Noonan said. "Which means we have to come up with our Plan B. My experience has shown . . ." Before he could continue, the Mephistophelian beast of the electronic universe began to throb in his breast pocket. "Speaking of the devil," he muttered as he read the name of the incoming caller on the miniscreen. He tapped the Beelzebubian disturber of the universe to life. "Commissioner Lizzard, what can I do for you?"

"Are you with that Navy man, Morals?"

"Morales," corrected Noonan as he nodded at Wynter. "Did you need to speak to him?"

"Morales. Yes, I knew he was something like that. Yes, can you put me on speakerphone?"

"Certainly," Noonan said and rolled his eyes at Wynter and Chelsea. He tapped the phone on speaker. Then he looked directly at Chelsea, pointed an index finger at her and raised it to his lips. Chelsea nodded.

"Ah, Mr. Morales." Lizzard's ingratiating voice came out of the ether. "It's good to meet you."

"Yes, sir." Wynter rolled his eyes. "What can the Navy do for the Department of Homeland Security?"

"I have just received a call from the legal people at the Navy, that is, your people, and they have instructed me to tell you and until this matter is settled, you are to work directly under me."

"Yes, sir." Wynter did not miss a beat. But he gave Noonan a 'told you so' look.

Lizzard continued as if Wynter was in breathless anticipation of what was coming next. "We have a situation here, all hush-hush, you understand, where there are some radicals who are planning on disrupting law and order and, of course, Homeland Security communications and actions in coastal North Carolina. Fortunately, we have a secret agent and are aware of their plans."

"Yes, sir." Wynter had a military bland expression.

"But we have a surprise for them. They believe, *via* our secret agent, that a major, radical funding source is going to come to their assistance. We are not going to dissuade them from that fantasy. So we have arranged for a pseudo-payment as bait. Once they take the bait, we'll have them. All of them, in the same trap."

"Yes, sir." Wynter was very good at this game.

"Now, Captain Morales, . . ."

"Petty Officer."

"Eh?" Lizzard's voice faltered.

"Petty Officer, Commissioner. I'm not a Captain. I'm a Petty Officer."

"Fine. Whatever," came the voice out of the ether. "Both of you, Captain and Petty Officer. We have a matter in play and each of you will have a part. Captain Noonan, you will be part of the Homeland Security force in Turtle where . . ."

Noonan expressed a false sense of surprise, "Turtle, sir? That's outside our jurisdiction."

"Not for Homeland Security, captain. When it comes to our nation's security there are no jurisdictional boundaries. Besides, Turtle does not have a police department because it is so small. You will be working with the North Carolina State Troopers. They have been notified they will serve as backup."

Noonan grimaced. "Yes, (pause) sir." There was just enough of a pause between the "yes" and "sir" to cause Wynter to raise his eyebrows. Chelsea's face was subordinate unreadable.

"The press will also be on hand, Captain, so I expect you to be cordial and provide as much information as possible to the press in this matter."

Noonan gave a quick look to the ceiling. "Press, (pause) sir. Are you sure this is a good idea. I mean, if these people are really dangerous, as you seem to indicate, (pause) sir, is it a good idea to have the press on hand?"

"Freedom of the Press, Captain. It's in the United States Constitution."

Wynter and Noonan gave each other a 'whaaaaatttt?' look while Chelsea continued her stony, expressionless, 'yes, sir, whatever' countenance.

"I see, (pause), sir. And this press person will meet us in Turtle?"

"Correct. He is the investigative reporter for the *Turtle Gazette*, a small, local paper. His name is Jerome Dawson Boone. He will be fully informed."

"And I am to work with Mr. Boone? To what extent?"

"To all extents, Captain. He will the eyes and ears of the public in this matter."

"Excuse me, Captain," Wynter cut in. "I'm familiar with the *Turtle Gazette* and it is, how shall I say it nicely, a weekly, local, advertisement-driven local paper. Why are you dealing with the *Turtle Gazette* rather than one of the largest papers in North Carolina or even the *Coastland Times*?"

"Secrecy, Captain."

"Petty Officer."

"Yes, Petty Officer. Secrecy. We don't want the bad boys and girls to know what we are doing."

"I see," said Wynter as he looked sideways at Noonan. "Let me sum up what you have told us."

"Excellent! A quick member of the team."

Noonan and Wynter were now stoic while Chelsea cracked a small smile – which lasted a nanosecond – and then her face was back to subservient bland.

"Yes, sir." Wynter did not pause between the "yes" and the "sir." "Captain Noonan and I are to coordinate with the North Carolina State Troopers in an event which will be happening in Turtle in the coming days."

"Tomorrow."

"Yes, sir." Again, no pause. "To recap to make sure I have this correctly. I am to work with Captain Noonan and the North Carolina State Troopers on a matter which will take place in Turtle tomorrow. We, Captain Noonan and I, are to work directly with the reporter from the *Turtle Gazette* and provide that person any and all information required to his story. Am I correct so far?"

"Excellent, Mr. Wynter."

Wynter didn't bother to correct Lizzard. He just plunged forward. "Captain Noonan will be on hand but the North Carolina State Troopers will be will command . . ." He didn't finish the sentence.

Lizzard cut in. "Command control will be in the hands of Homeland Security. I and Commissioner Boris Hernandez will be onsite and we will take overall command. Your role and that of Captain Noonan will be to support our actions."

"Yes, sir." Wynter was as Navy as Navy can be. Again no pause between "yes" and "sir." Wynter looked sideways at Chelsea. "As a suggestion, Commissioner, it might be a good idea to have *more* police on the scene than is necessary. In Navy jargon, it is known as overpower. You never know if you will need more personnel than planned. I'd suggest we request backup from another police department. Say, the Pamlico City Police Department. A few extra police at the scene will be added security. Besides, if Captain Noonan and I are going to have to lead a convoy of troopers to Turtle, one or two more vehicles from Pamlico City will not arouse any suspicion."

"An excellent suggestion, Mr. Wynter! Captain Noonan, you should take an example from Mr. Wynter's farsightedness! Yes, an excellent idea. Captain Noonan, please contact the Pamlico City Police Department for a few officers for special duty tomorrow."

"Of course, (pause) sir." Noonan smiled and gave Wynter a 'you clever dog' look.

"Well, that seems to have wrapped everything up nicely. Captain Noonan, Mr. Wynter. Please be ready to travel to Turtle at midnight. Tonight. I will be in touch with you before then to tell you where to meet the convoy."

"When will this matter actually come to a head?" Wynter asked.

"The actual timing is in flux, Captain. All plans are in place at this time. Commissioner Hernandez has arranged for the delivery of an item from Manteo that will be used in the matter. It will be leaving at an undisclosed early hour and be in Turtle well before nine a.m."

"And this matter will take place in Turtle at nine a.m. tomorrow, sir?" Wynter sounded perfectly young-and-ambitious.

"Correct. All of the moving pieces must be in place by nine a.m."

Noonan kind of shook his head and then smiled at Chelsea before he cut in. "And I will coordinate with the Pamlico City Police Department for backup."

Lizzard was excited. "Our team in action! Wonderful. We will then see what we will see. Everything will start at midnight. I will be in touch. Do not be a moment late. And remember, this is all hush-hush."

With that the voice in the ether went off. Noonan tapped the speaker button and waited for the iPhone screen to go to default before he looked up at Chelsea. "Seems you've just had a rapid recovery."

"I'm feeling better already," Chelsea said with a smile. "And I can hardly wait for nine a.m. tomorrow and," faking Lizzard's voice, "I won't be a moment late."

As they all stood up to leave, Noonan stopped them for a moment. "I suggest we all look in our boxes of tricks for anything we might and could need for this assignment. We have absolutely no idea what's going to happen but I want to be prepared for any contingency."

"You mean like binoculars and pocket knives?" Chelsea asked.

"Anything," Noonan replied. "And everything. All we know for sure is gold is involved. It has to be moved and that will take time. Gold is heavy. Once the game starts, we will not have the luxury of time to get something we need. Let's just bring it with us; walkie-talkies, handcuffs, magnifying glasses, duct tape, vinegar."

"Vinegar?" Chelsea gave Noonan an odd look."

"To tell real gold from fake gold," Noonan said. "An old trick. If you put real gold in vinegar for a few minutes it shines. Fake gold changes color with acid."

"I didn't know that. Are we going to get a few minutes to test any gold?"

Noonan shook his head. "I don't know. All I know is that we are only going to get one bite out of this apple."

# CHAPTER 41

Turtle, even by North Carolina standards, was a very small town. Very small. And small towns anywhere in America have one thing in common: everyone knows everyone else's business. From dipsomania to abortions, inheritance to vandalism and who's been messin' with hims, hers or thems. There were no secrets in Turtle.

So, when Jerome Dawson Boone got a call at Turtle Elementary **from Homeland Security** via the *Turtle Gazette*, well, as they say in small towns, tongues began wagging. What was this all about?

No one had to add one and one to get two. They didn't need a two. Everybody knew something was up. What was going to happen tomorrow? Saturday. In Turtle? Get real! Nothing ever happened in Turtle. And not on a Saturday.

But there was that call *from Homeland Security.*

Then things took a rather nasty turn.

Six kiddos disappeared after school.

And the bus they were in was gone too.

WWWWWhhhhhaaaattt???!!!!!!

Special education kiddos vanishing into thin air.

Along with their bus.

Kidnapping?

Be real!

No one in Turtle had any money.

So why kidnap kids? And special education kids at that.

Was there a link?

Then there was that call **from Homeland Security.**

114

By eight Friday evening the missing kiddos were as big a story in Turtle as the call **from Homeland Security.** Just in case the two were connected – and could they not be connected? – Boone was besieged with calls from concerned parents, collaterals and extended family members of the six kiddos. Just their names were a mix of Americana: Jerome Abramowitz, Sheila Mugavi, Abdula Channing, Camilla Hernandez, Chloe Adrondak and Darius Abd Al-Quadir. In the 21ˢᵗ Century, America was truly the ethnic melting pot of the world.

# CHAPTER 42

It was three a.m. when Michael Patterson slid open the loading dock door of Patterson Precious Metals. Four North Carolina State Troopers transferred the 800 pounds of gold from melted jewelry, ingot and coins from the vault into the back of an armored car. The transfer took less than five minutes.

Then the armored car was off, escorted by a contingent of marked and unmarked North Carolina State Troopers vehicles. The convoy made it to Turtle in three-quarters of an hour. The armored car and North Carolina State Trooper contingent skirted the outskirts of the city, which was not hard, and entered the widespread webbing of the railyards from the west. The convoy bounced over a dozen abandoned rail lines before coming to a massive mechanical shed door. It was one of a half-dozen doors, evidence that in its prime the Turtle railyards, then known as Terminus – was the heartbeat of the North Carolina coastal transportation network. Now the rail yard was a decaying vestige of a golden past.

The double doors of the mechanical shed swing open and the armored car and trooper cars backed into the vacuous room.

There were a double set of tracks inside the warehouse. At one time there had been so much repair work the shed had to be operational 24/7. The double tracks allowed for double the amount of work to be completed at the same time. As one rail car or locomotive was repaired, it was shuttled out of the mechanical shed to make room for the next incoming flat car, boxcar, locomotive, or hand cart. The double tracks allowed for two rail cars to be worked on at the same time and neither would have to move to allow another car out of the mechanical shed.

Double tracks meant two repair teams could work at the same time in the same shed with the same tools.

The armored car was backed up to an empty flatcar. The 60-pound ingots were unloaded, one at a time, and placed on the flatcar. Then the pile was covered with a canvas sheet secured with straps. When the last of the gold was transferred from the back of the armored vehicle to the flat car, the armored car was ordered out of the mechanical shed.

But it did not go back to Manteo.

It went to a designated North Carolina State Trooper parking area well beyond the outskirts of Turtle. Here it would sit – with its two drivers – until the gold was to be moved back to Patterson Precious Metals in Manteo.

No phone calls were allowed.

No computers were allowed.

The drivers did not care. They were on night-time and double-time wages. They were not complaining.

All they were required to do was drive. They did not have to load the gold. They did not have to unload the gold. They did not have to worry about being robbed because they were being escorted by a convoy of North Carolina State Troopers. In force. So, they did not have to be observant. So, they were not. If they had been, they would have noticed another flat car in the mechanical shed. This one had a small load on its back, identical in size to the 800 pounds of gold on the flat car the State Troopers had just loaded on another flatcar.

# CHAPTER 43

The appearance of Archie Scarborough at the Manteo office of Homeland Security was not unexpected.

His message was.

Everything had been going along swimmingly for Lizzard and Hernandez. There had not been a single hitch. The flash drive surreptitiously supplied by Scarborough had been reviewed by both Lizzard and Hernandez and sent up the administrative chain of command. Yes, the muckety mucks in Washington D. C. had said it would be necessary to keep a very close eye on ACTION FOR AMERICA. As a matter of fact, Homeland Security had them on the hate-watch list. As did the Southern Poverty Law Center. They were even listed in yellow on the Southern Poverty Law Center Hate Map. One of more than 900 hate groups the Law Center kept watch. If you were a red group – red as in the color of the circle on the Law Center's map of hatred – you were benign in the sense that you just hated people but didn't do much about it. Yellow was a different category. Yellow was for hate groups who were active. Their activities included marches, rallies, handouts that pushed the concept of Freedom of Speech so far that even extreme liberals felt queasy and criminal acts. (Why yellow was for the dangerous groups, and red for the benign was never explained. Common sense indicated the colors should have been reversed.)

Interestingly, the Southern Poverty Law Center hate map also had green groups which had no overall category designation. The Green designation included such groups as the Fundamentalist Latter-Day Saints, Holy Nation of Odin, A2z Publications, Repent Amarillo, and

National Prayer Network. In addition to the anti-Muslim groups, there were black separatists, anti-LBGT associations, and sort-of, kind-of religious organizations. Only Alaska and Hawaii had no hate groups listed.

ACTION FOR AMERICA had been a green group until Lizzard and Hernandez began forwarding the inside information up the chain of command. Clearly, there had been some communication with the Southern Poverty Law Center because the association went from green to red and then yellow in a matter of four months. As the plans of ACTION FOR AMERICA began to hint of disruption of the waterways and contamination of the drinking water supplies from the rivers of coastal North Carolina, the United States Coast Guard was brought into the scheme of surveillance. Commissioners Lizzard and Hernandez were designated as the point of contact for any and all operation details.

Then came an oddity of the operation. Homeland Security for North Carolina was a rat's nest of intertwined, interlocking, convoluted lines of operation, authority and funding. It involved coordination with all branches of the military in the area, State Troopers, local police, United States Coast Guard, weather service, communications companies large and small, public and private utilities along with city, county, and state governments. While Homeland Security operated efficiently at the national level – national, meaning the Washington D. C. Office – and only the Washington D. C. office – at every subordinate level, it was a headless organization. Or, more accurately, it was a *head-of-plenty* operation. Every thread of the rat's nest had a next-in-command which did not include Homeland Security. Thus the office of the Coastal North Carolina Commissioner of Homeland Security was the center of a communication network of agencies, offices, and operations who did not recognize the Coastal North Carolina offices of Homeland Security as being in charge of anything except self-inflicted chaos.

But, as Alaskan humorist Warren Sitka notes, "Chaos is the mother's milk of opportunity."

Though neither Lizzard nor Hernandez were Alaskan, they were well aware of the golden opportunity chaos had presented them. It gave them freedom of action without responsibility. Every memo moving its way up the various chains of command was given a lip service response because every other office was cced so no one office had the responsibility of saying yes, no or more information required.

No one was taking them seriously.

And, since no agency, office or operation in the network told them "no," the two commissioners were free to do as they pleased.

So they did.

As no agency told them "no" to the "acquisition of material to pursue additional information as to the plans of ACTION FOR AMERICA," Lizzard and Hernandez simply used United States government purchase orders to acquire the 800 pounds of gold along with the 800 pounds of *faux* gold.

The two commissioners were not worried. Theirs was going to be a classic bait-and-switch operation. With the help of stage magician Archie Scarborough, the two commissioners were going to let the ACTION FOR AMERICA conspirator check out the 800 pounds of real gold from Patterson's Precious Metals. Then, while the conspirator's proverbial back was turned, the commissioners would switch the real gold for the fake gold. It was simply a matter of prestidigitation. The conspirator would go off with the fake gold to join with his fellow conspirators. They would gather to buy and use the TAPT and when the rats were all in the same trap, **_BANG_**, the North Carolina State Troopers and Homeland Security would swoop in and make a spectacular arrest.

With a press person in tow.

Which the twin commissioners would tout as proof of their due diligence in 'Keeping the Nation Safe.'

And not an ounce of gold will have been lost. It would be under guard of the North Carolina State Troopers every foot of the way every second of the operation, from Patterson's Precious Metals to the *faux* exchange in the railroad warehouse in Turtle and then back to Patterson's vault for safekeeping.

No harm, no foul.

Maybe, just maybe, that all changed when Archie Scarborough showed up with the ransom note from ACTION FOR AMERICA.

And when Rodolpho Sacerdote, the faceless, nameless, double agent, inside contact implant in ACTION FOR AMERICA, was contacted, he expressed complete surprise. He said he knew nothing about any kidnapping. All he was doing was acting as an informant for the Office of Homeland Security which was only involved in a bait-and-switch with 800 pounds of gold. He said he would "call around" to see if he could find out what was going on but, as far as he was concerned, he was "staying out of the way" while the Office of Homeland Security was snatching the extortionists.

# CHAPTER 44

"You know," Chelsea said as the three were outbound to Turtle. "I like and do not like what is happenings. On the one hand, we are being swept down a river not of our choosing. On the other hand, we have to come up with a Plan B without knowing what it is, exactly, we are being swept toward."

Wynter smiled. "Well, you know why you should always hire an economist with one hand?"

Chelsea was not amused. "I don't know where this is going, but, OK, why do you only hire an economist with one hand."

"Because then he can never say, 'on the other hand.'"

Noonan gave a chuckle. "I haven't heard that before. But I feel for you, Chelsea. We don't know what's happening. Exactly, anyway. But there is one thing I know for certain. If it is possible for things to go awry they will particularly if the Department of Homeland Security is involved. Those people are not law enforcement. They are political. Political people do not concentrate on the end game. They only look forward to the next opportunity for publicity. They only plan for the publicity. Once the news cameras are shut off, the event is like the Hittites: history."

"I hear you," Wynter snorted. "But we're stuck with the long haul. Anything I do, we, you two and me, do, goes into our personnel file. Every mistake I have ever made has come back to haunt me time after time. Mistakes I make are never forgotten. And when I do something right, the credit goes right up the chain of command. It is like I do not exist."

"OK," Noonan chuckled. "Let's cut the small talk and concentrate on the end game. We know there is going to be some kind of bait-

and-switch with 800 pounds of gold. It's going to be a pretty simple bait-and-switch because Homeland Security is involved. John Law is involved as backup which means we're most likely going to be around to make sure if something goes wrong all the exits are covered. That's the way John Law thinks. Or, at least, that's probably what Homeland Security has been told. I'm sure Lizzard and Hernandez said something along the lines of 'Yeah, yeah, yeah, take care of it.' And that's as far as Lizzard and Hernandez thought."

"That was probably as far as the State Troopers could go," Chelsea cut in. "Chain of command and all. That's probably the best they could get. So they probably did what I would do: set up roadblocks just in case something went wrong. Maybe do something about the rail lines out of Turtle. I'd also call the Coast Guard about putting some small boats in water if there are usable rivers or streams around Turtle. But that's as far as I could go."

"A good plan," Noonan said scratching his head. "But the bad boys and girls know that's what we, John Law, are going to do. They anticipate what we are going to do. So they are going to do something different. We have two advantages over Homeland Security . . ."

"Three," put in Wynter. "We are thinking ahead of the game. They are not."

"Good point," Noonan congratulated Wynter. "Three, yes. The other two are 1) we know they are going to do something unexpected and 2) gold is heavy. Eight hundred pounds is not something you can put in your pocket and walk out the door with. That kind of poundage requires a vehicle. If the vehicle has to go through a roadblock, the gold has to be well hidden. Be undetectable."

"More likely it will be in several vehicles," Chelsea cut in. "I don't see them putting 800 pounds in one vehicle. That's a lot of weight."

"Not really," Wynter said thoughtfully. "Four football players can fit in an SUV with no problem."

"Of course," Chelsea countered. "But the problem is not the weight; it's the space. The North Carolina State Troopers are no slouches. When they check cars and trucks at a roadblock, they are going to be looking for 800 pounds of gold. That means opening trunks, lifting back seats, the whole nine yards. There are not going to be that many vehicles coming through the roadblocks, I mean, we're talking about traffic out of Turtle, for God's sake."

"True," Noonan noted. "But the bad boys and girls have already solved that problem. What we have to do is think outside of the box, off the wall, so to speak. And we have to do it quickly because whatever they have planned is already in motion. They know what they are going to do and the clock is ticking. When the moment of the bait-and-switch goes wrong, we have to have an inkling of what is going to happen. We are only going to get one shot at this."

"We'd better make it a good one," Wynter said. "Because if we don't hit the nail on the head, it'll be in our personnel files f-o-r-e-v-e-r-."

# CHAPTER 45

It was not an unexpected event when the arrest squad arrived at the headquarters of ACTION FOR AMERICA. It was not unexpected because in the murky world of the almost-underbelly of society, 'the government' was always one step away from 'shutting us down.' Thus the raid was not unexpected. 'Just in case' plans were in place but, frankly, the leaders were more prone to speak of the 'impending raid' than actually preparing for it.

The truth be said, there were not a lot of 'sensitive documents' that would be of value to 'the government.' Or, as ACTION FOR AMER-ICA activists pronounced it, 'govermint.' As there were few 'sensitive documents' there was no reason to rush to a shredder in the backroom as 'jackbooted agents of the government' were coming in the front door.

What did surprise the inner circle cabal of ACTION FOR AMER-ICA was the wealth of password-gated, encrypted documentation taken off their computer which they swore they had never seen and did not know existed.

# CHAPTER 46

When it came to special education, there was only one thing that had improved over the previous three or four decades. In the old days, special education kids were sequestered. They were kept away from the 'normal' children and proceeded through life as invisible participants of the citizenship process.

This all changed with mainstreaming. Now the special education students were part of the educational process in the sense they were in the schools. This did three things at once, all of them positive. First, it was a clear message to the 'normal' students that the individuals in the special education program were not pariahs. They were part of 'us,' rather than outliers of civilization. Even better, many schools had mentoring requirements where 'normal' students would participate with the special education students during class time, physical education, life skills and after-hour activities.

The second benefit of mainstreaming was the freedom it gave to parents. In the 'bad old days' the special education schedule was, at best, erratic. Students were either institutionalized in the sense they went into institutions and never came out or were babysat all day. And the concept of 'all day' depended on state funding, not the schedule of the parents. But with mainstreaming, parents were assured their special education children had a set schedule which meant the parents could get regular jobs. Instead of being at the whim of either the schedule of the institutional babysitters or the state budget, parents were confident their children would start school at about 9 am and be home for supper.

This meant both parents could work, adding money to the household, tax income to the state and economic turnover in the community.

Third, special education trifurcated. There was Special Education which included those kiddos who were never going to improve or had little chance of becoming productive citizens. They were the saddest of the lot. For them, there was no chance of 'moving on.' They would be in wheelchairs for their entire life. If cognizant of the world, they might thrash violently at the slightest provocation, be a six-year-old in the body of an adult, have no control of their bodily functions, pretend to be dead rather than participate in any activity including lunch or be oblivious to all external stimuli. They would be as likely to climb a bookcase as hide under a table for no reason whatsoever. They might be fed through a tube directly into their stomach, have a violent addictive reactions to peanuts, seeing things (maybe) that others could not detect with their eyes. If they could be lured into conventional games, they might try to force a jigsaw puzzle part to fit even to the point of tearing it or throw all the cards in a deck into the air looking for the one card wanting even though they were not sure which card it was that was lacking. Some would spit on the floor and then lick it up, bite for no apparent reason, be a 'runner' the moment the special education room door was unlocked or go ballistic for a reason or no reason.

The second tier was generally called Life Skills. Life Skills kiddos were those who could be productive in society with hands-on management. These included a wide range of mental difficulties. The point of Life Skills was adaptive education and behavior. These students would become somewhat productive members of society but would still require ongoing mentoring. In the jargon of the old days, they were "slow" but not "stupid."

The third tier was euphemistically called Resource. These were students who were not mentally impaired but had emotional problems. Or attitudes which precluded them from learning. Or they could not cope with the requirements of everyday life. Euphemistically, they were 'troubled youth with low-esteem with both disciplinary and behavior issues.' In many cases, they were self-inflicting victims who could, would, might become productive members of society when they worked out the mental kinks in their personality. These kiddos included boys who were just marking time until they turned 17 ½ so they could join the army or girls who were simply planning on getting married and having children so 'education had no purpose.'

Life Skills and Resource kiddos understood the rhythm of life. Special Education students did not and this made them vulnerable to the exigencies of life. It also made them made of gold for someone to exploit not them, but those who loved them. And this was exactly what had happened.

# CHAPTER 47

There was not an empty chair in the abandoned railway terminal in Turtle. This, however, was not unusual. That was because there were no chairs in the terminal. There had not been chairs in that building for a good two decades. The last time a chair had been in the room was just before the one-room elementary school moved across town to its current location adjacent to the Turtle City Hall.

There were no chairs so everyone stood.

It was not a particularly pleasant meeting.

It was not a particularly pleasant meeting because it was not clear to anyone – cops, troopers or civilians – why they were there. None of them, save the commissioners, had any idea what they were doing in a vacant warehouse in the middle of what in North Carolina was 'nowhere.' It had all been, to quote the commissioners of Homeland Security for Sandersonville and Coastal North Carolina, "hush hush," and that was the way the commissioners wanted it. Hush-hush and need to know only. So, everyone in the room, had been ordered to be there by someone 'up the administrative food chain' and everyone in the room had absolutely no idea why they were there.

"This has bad news written all over it," Noonan said to Chelsea and Wynter under his breath.

Since the chain of command snaked up through Homeland Security, the men and women in blue had no choice but to follow the directions laid out by the commissioners. No one liked it; but orders were orders.

All this being said, no one had any idea why they had been dragged out of bed in the middle of the night to follow an armored car to the outskirts of a town so small you missed it if you blinked. Yet, here they were, in an empty warehouse, standing and waiting for instruction from two men who had last worn a uniform at a Boy Scout Jamboree in the last century.

At the front of the room was a Formica table just long enough for three people. Lizzard and Hernandez were huddled behind the table with a young man Noonan had never seen. Why Lizzard would share the spotlight with anyone was beyond Noonan – until Lizzard introduced the man as Jerome Dawson Boone, Investigative Reporter for the *Turtle Gazette*.

The fetid smell of politics assaulted Noonan's nostrils.

"I didn't know Turtle had a *newspaper*, much less an investigative reporter," Chelsea said under her breath.

"It doesn't have either," replied Noonan quietly. "The *Turtle Gazette* is a weekend shopper with an occasional article of local interest."

"Then what's he doing here?" Chelsea indicated Boone with the slight raise of her right shoulder.

"Your man Lizzard must love publicity," Wynter said under his breath. "Hernandez surely does. That's why we're in this mess."

Before the three could continue to share impressions, Lizzard hammered the meeting to order, so to speak, with a three-ring binder. There was instant silence.

"For those of you who do not know me," Lizzard began with an imperial raising of his right arm, "I am Commissioner of Homeland Security for Sandersonville, Edward Lizzard III. (He emphasized the III.)

"I and my colleague," he indicated Hernandez, "have been appointed by the home office of Homeland Security," (pause) "in Washington, D. C. (pause) "to form the North Carolina Homeland Security task force. We have a crisis here in coastal North Carolina and fortunately," (pause), "we will be able to nip the plan in the bud."

Someone in the audience said something about jurisdiction and Hernandez cut the man off. "When it comes to homeland security, there are no jurisdictional boundaries. We are here to protect America in all cities, counties, and states."

No one said anything. This was not to assume that nothing was to be said, just that no one said anything. It was the typical silence of a department meeting. Everyone was required to be there and no one said anything because the faster the meeting was over the faster everyone could go back to doing something that was productive. Or anything. Productive or not. So you just shut your mouth, listened and asked no questions.

Lizzard leaped into the enforced silence. "Homeland Security has been dealing *sub rosa* with ACTION FOR AMERICA, a white supremacist group operating in North Carolina." He said the term *sub rosa* with an accent and kind of/sort of raised the right finger of his right hand to his mouth to indicate some manner of silence. "ACTION FOR AMERICA is, at this time, planning a major disruption here in coastal North Carolina. It involves the destruction of telephone lines, hacking of the telecommunications systems from Virginia Beach, a raid on the federal armory in Greenville and burning of a mosque in Durham along with six black churches. The rats, so to speak, have gathered in a conclave outside of Greenville. They are waiting for $15 million in gold, the gold which you escorted here to Turtle.

There was an audible gasp in the room. A lot of someones started to say many things but Hernandez cut them off with a tap of his three-ring binder. "Time is very short, ladies and gentlemen, very short. This is not a war game and this is not an exercise. This is the real McCoy. Homeland Security has been dealing *sub rosa*" – he said the term in the same hushed manner as Lizzard and made the same motion with his right index finger – "for several months. We have covered all the bases. To catch all the rats in the same trap we need bait. Real bait. For that reason, we arranged to purchase 800 pounds of gold to convince ACTION FOR AMERICA that we, through our *sub rosa* agent" – against the hushed tone and forefinger – "are offering to the terrorists. That 800 pounds of gold is what you have escorted here. The terrorists want the 800 pounds of gold to be loaded onto a flatcar for removal down the tracks to Greenville. There the gold will be parceled out to the conspirators. That's when we will close in. We will catch all the rats in the same trap."

This time there was no moment of silence.

"We're giving terrorists 800 pounds of gold?!" It was from a senior state trooper who was so well-placed his name tag was still on his breast pocket. "That's illegal. I don't care if you are with Homeland Security. Giving money to terrorist is flat-out illegal. (Pause) Not to mention putting every one of us here," he extended his arm and swept the room, "at risk for a felony charge. This is not . . "

Lizzard cut him off. "We hear you, Commander. But you didn't let us finish. We are not giving ACTION FOR AMERICA gold. We are letting the terrorist verify the gold we have is authentic and then we are going to pull a bait-and-switch. After the terrorist examines the gold on the flat car, we are going to give him a flatcar of fake gold, painted lead bricks. He'll think he has the real gold."

This did not satisfy the state trooper. "That's a very, very, very risky business. How are you going to make sure that the real gold doesn't get snagged?"

"Actually," Hernandez was snidely optimistic, "that's your job. Right now, as you know, the gold is on a flatcar in a mechanical shed. The fake gold is hidden on a flat car in the same shed. Where, where, where," Hernandez said as he shushed the gathering with his hands as if he were pushing the objections back. "Where, where it is right now. Under guard. As you know, because your men are guarding it. Both flatcars. The terrorist will examine the real gold and when he steps outside to contact his fellow conspirators, we will switch the flat cars. The terrorist will leave with the fake gold and the real gold will stay in the mechanical shed. As soon as the terrorist is well away from Turtle, you and your fellow officers will off-load the real gold from the flatcar and escort the real gold back to the Homeland Security holding facilities in Manteo."

Even this did not satisfy someone in the gathering. "You don't think the terrorist will know there's probably going to be a bait-and-switch?"

Lizzard smiled slyly. "We've got the best people working with us. The best. People who have been in the magic business for decades. It will go off without a hitch. If there's a glitch, we will still have the real gold. We've got your people surrounding the mechanical shed. That will keep ACTION FOR AMERICA from pulling a double-cross. The real gold is on the flatcar in the mechanical shed. We've got two dozen men and women in blue around the shed. All they have to do is stay out of sight for five minutes, the amount of time it will take for the terrorist to examine the real gold, call his fellow conspirators and then leave with the fake gold. Then the real gold goes back to Manteo."

"That's a lot of gold," someone said. "We're talking, what $15 million. Who's watching who here? I mean, that's enough to turn a few heads, even if they are wearing blue. Sticky fingers, you know." Then someone let the sentence hang.

"True," cut in Hernandez. "While we don't believe that is a possibility, we, at Homeland Security, double-check every lock and double-lock every door. As remote as that possibility is, yes, we have taken that possibility into account. That's why we have shuffled all personnel."

There was a buzz, and it was not a pleasant one. Before Hernandez had finished speaking the State Trooper Commander was on his feet. "That is, is, not a good idea. It's, it's uncoordinated. There will be no way for all our people to stay coordinated. By that, I mean that the State Troopers have their own communication network which is separate from Homeland Security. And there are some Sandersonville Police here and some Pamlico City Police who have their own communication network. If anything goes wrong, it's going to be a rats nest of communication links and lines."

Lizzard shook his head a smiled. "It will never come to that. The gold is secure now. It will be secure after ACTION FOR AMERICA takes the fake gold. Then you," his index finger swept the gathering, "will take the gold back to the Homeland Security vault. The gold is never going to leave the mechanical shed. You," again he swept the gathering with his index finger, "are going to make sure of that. That's your job. This is basically a bait-and-switch operation. You will be watching the real gold the whole time. If things start to go bad, we'll shut down the entire operation. The gold on the flatcar in the mechanical shed is not going anywhere. All you," and once again, his index finger swept the sea of blue, "have to do is stay hidden while the terrorist examines the gold. The gold doesn't move, period. The terrorist comes in, checks the gold, you keep your heads down. The fake gold goes out, you watch the real gold. When we," Lizzard pointed at Hernandez and himself, "give you the word, you radio the armored car. It goes into the mechanical shed, you load the gold back into the armored car and escort it back to Manteo. Everything will be done by noon and you can take the rest of the day off."

There was a lot of grumbling and Lizzard dismissed the gathering.

As Noonan, Wynter, and Chelsea were about to leave, Lizzard waved them aside. "Not you, Captain Noonan. I need you up here with you associates."

# CHAPTER 48

Archie Scarborough was in a rage.
Possibly for very good reason.
But then again, . . .

"Mr. Scarborough," the North Carolina State Trooper was politically correct to be polite, but she was a cop. She knew a con when he saw one. Smelled him, actually. This man, this Archie Scarborough was a con. But he was a slippery con. He was the kind of a con who never got caught. Plenty of could have and probably did but when it came to the hard evidence, zip, *nada, niento.*

Suspicion was not enough. Documentation, forensics, eyewitness and confessions, AH!, that was the proof of the pudding. Gut feelings were good for Detective First, Second, and Third Class but zip, *nada and niento* when it came to the courtroom.

"Let me make sure I understand exactly what you are saying," the trooper looked at her notes. "Mr. Scarborough,. . ."

"Archie. I'm Archie."

"If we're at the chamber of commerce, Archie will be sufficient. Here, on tape, in the interrogation room, we're formal. Now, Mr. Scarborough, I want to make sure I have your story straight. You had never heard of or met the man who handed you this note." She pointed to a sheet of paper in a plastic bag.

"That is somewhat correct," Scarborough waffled. "I do a lot of business with a lot of people, directly and indirectly. And I'm a participator and supporter of many public service organizations. Could I have had some interaction with anyone from ACTION FOR AMERICA before this unknown person gave me the note? Possibly. Do I remember any meeting of substance, no. Did he look familiar? Yes, no, and maybe."

"But you have no contact with him regarding these children?"

"None regarding the children. He just showed up and handed me the note. Said, take it to the State Troopers."

"Why would he do that?"

"NAC, or, what we said where I grew up, 'Not a Clue.'"

"Mr. Scarborough, I find it hard to believe that a total stranger would show up in your place of business and give a ransom note to someone who has nothing to do with the children involved. Do you see my problem?"

"Absolutely. My guess is that he knew I was dealing with the Office of Homeland Security and knew it was collecting 800 pounds of gold for some purpose."

"So, you think they approached you because of the gold?"

"No other reason to approach me. Like you said, I have no connection with the children. Any of them."

"Well, why didn't he go to the Office of Homeland Security, If they had the gold and you didn't, it would make sense to go to them with the ransom demand."

"Maybe. The problem? There is no link between the gold and Homeland Security and the kidnapped children. All I know of the gold is it is being used in some kind of a hush-hush operation, Homeland Security's words, not mine. But I am the link between the gold and the Office of Homeland Security. So, logically, to get a message to the Office of Homeland Security, who has the gold, the perpetrators can go through me."

"Well, Mr. Scarborough, if that's the case, why did you bring the ransom note to the North Carolina State Troopers. Why not give the note to the Office of Homeland Security?

Scarborough looked around as if to see who else was listening. It was a vain effort for three reasons. First, he knew he was being filmed. Second, he knew who was in the room with him. Third, it was to imply he was about to tell a secret which the North Carolina State Troopers was not going to believe. "Well, (pause) officer. Homeland Security is, well, you know, not a law enforcement operation. I'm not sure what they are. But if push comes to shove, officer, and something goes wrong, I don't want anyone saying that I did not give the critical information I had to the proper authorities. Law enforcement people, you know." Scarborough quoted "law enforcement people" in the air with his fingers.

The trooper was not taken by the theatrics. "OK. Let me ask the question in another way. Other than a possible occasional meeting with someone from ACTION FOR AMERICA, have you had or do you have an ongoing arrangement with them or anyone associated with them?"

"I do not want to answer 'no' to that question and then find out one of their members booked a fishing expedition or has an account at my store under a business name. So, let me answer in my own way. Specifically regarding the Homeland Security matter, and only the Homeland Security matter of which I am unsure what I can reveal, I do not have a contact with ACTION FOR AMERICA or anyone I know to be a member of that association. I believe I was given the ransom note because it is common knowledge in the community – and particularly anyone who is associated with the jewelry or precious metal industries – that I have been instrumental with an effort to acquire a certain poundage of gold for Homeland Security. I am advising, but not working with, the Office of Homeland Security on the dispensation of that gold. It is therefore logical to assume that ACTION FOR AMERICA believed me to be the portal to submit this ransom letter." He pointed at the note. "I have no children. I know no special education children and I have no connection with the Turtle School District or the City of Turtle."

# CHAPTER 49

In 1784, while serving as a lieutenant in the British Royal Artillery, Henry Shrapnel created what he dubbed a "spherical case." It was a hollow cannonball filled with lead shot and an explosive core. When fired from a cannon, the ball would explode in midair and spray the enemy with fragmented lead shot. It was field-tested in Gibraltar in 1787 to the great satisfaction of the chain of command. Sixty years after his death, Shrapnel was honored, so to speak, by having his name associated with the deadly fragmentation. Since then, Shrapnel's shrapnel has been added to the dictionary.

Shrapnel is the best term to use in the description of what happened to the Homeland Security law enforcement contingent in Turtle which had been assigned to backstop the special operation. From the law enforcement perspective, Homeland Security was a low priority. It was not an on-the-ground operation. More accurately, it was pie in the sky. Homeland Security did not operate in the weeds. It operated because of federal funding. As long as there were dollars available, Homeland Security would 'uncover' boogeymen. When it came to law enforcement dollars, there would always be bad men and bad women with the 'lean and hungry look.'

Even more important, the gasoline in the tank of Homeland Security was publicity. When the blast of publicity faded, so did the interest of the Office of Homeland Security. For law enforcement, the reality with quite the opposite. It was rare for the completion of a case to receive any publicity at all and rarely a commendation. Holding down the crime rate was the job of law enforcement. Thus, whatever law enforcement did, it was 'part of the job' and not subject to commendation or praise in the local press. When either came it was welcomed, but not expected.

However – and this was a *monstrous* however – the repercussions from any law and order failure to respond to a law enforcement matter were long-lasting. One missed clue could ruin a career. Even more important, law enforcement publicity was universally bad. When a 'bad event' occurred, the first reaction of the press and public was to laser focus on the forces of law and order with a single spoken and unspoken question: "Well, what are YOU doing about it?!"

The ransom letter from ACTION FOR AMERICA struck the law enforcement community like a spiderweb of disaster in cloud-to-ground lightning sheet. Personnel support for Homeland Security was looked upon as odious but politically required duty. Kidnapping was an entirely different matter. It required on-the-ground action NOW. NOW was NOW and personnel from the North Carolina State Troopers, Sandersonville Police Department, and the Pamlico Police Department scattered like shrapnel from an exploding mortar. Within the time length of an accelerated heartbeat, three coordinated, coordinating command centers erupted to life. Homeland Security be damned.

# CHAPTER 50

Whatever commissioners Lizzard and Hernandez were originally going to say to Noonan, Wynter and Chelsea were lost in the scattering of law enforcement personnel. Instantaneous to the announcement that a school bus with children was being held hostage, the abandoned railway terminal in Turtle emptied like PFCs at a commander's call. There was only a momentary stall while supervisors assigned the lowest level officers of the law to 'remain on duty here.' After that, all that remained in the terminal was an echo.

Noonan, Wynter, and Chelsea stood firm as rocks in the retreating tide of blue. When the moment passed, there were less than a dozen officers, none above the rank of patrolman first-class and three North Carolina State Troopers who were young enough to need someone else to buy their cigarettes.

"This is a fine mess we are in," Wynter said under his breath as the three advanced on the table.

"Someone has planned well," Noonan responded.

Lizzard and Hernandez were clearly shocked. At least that was what showed on their face. Their words belied their concern.

"Well, things have not changed. Captain Noonan, I don't believe you have met the Commissioner for Homeland Security for the Coastal North Carolina." Simultaneously Hernandez extended his hand. Lizzard continued, "And this is Jerome Dawson Boone, investigative reporter for the *Turtle Gazette*. He is here to document and report on the progress of our enterprise." Boone could not extend a hand as his chest was covered with cameras on lanyards. Some of the cameras had telephoto lenses and the combined weight of the instruments caused him to lean slightly forward.

"Commissioner," Noonan was cautious in his statement. "It appears things have changed substantially in the last few moments. We," he indicated Wynter and Chelsea, "need to know as soon as possible what your plans are. We have lost most of the support of law enforcement and that puts us at an extreme disadvantage."

Lizzard's eyes lied when he said, "Oh, no. Nothing has changed. The plan is still in place. We'll just have to make do it with fewer people. You and Captain Morals here," Lizzard pointed at Wynter – and Wynter did not correct the title or pronunciation of his last name – will just have to do double duty. And you, you," Lizzard struggled to remember Chelsea's name, first and last.

"Chelsea Edison. Pamlico Police Department. On assignment with Captain Noonan and Chief Petty Officer Morales." She gave Wynter's correct rank and pronounced his name correctly. Lizzard gave no indication he had made a double mistake.

"From the Dematerializing Armored Car Case, right? We got a lot of publicity for that matter. Yes, indeed."

Chelsea said nothing.

"Nice to have you here."

"Now that the niceties over, Commissioner," Noonan prodded Lizzard, "We need to know as soon as possible what the plan is and how we fit in."

"The plan, *Captain* Noonan," Lizzard said, emphasizing the word *Captain*, "has not changed. You, the three of you, will just have to do double-duty. In a nutshell, a radical right-wing group, ACTION FOR AMERICA, plans to disrupt the transportation and mailing systems of Coastal North Carolina. To do so they need money and that money is in the form of gold."

"Why gold?" Wynter asked.

Lizzard gave the traditional old-tired-don't-you-know-anything look and then said. "Because gold is untraceable. Gold is gold. ACTION FOR AMERICA wanted gold because it is untraceable. That's why we gathered 800 pounds of the metal. It's sitting on a flatcar in the mechanical shed over there." He pointed through the wall of the terminal at an imaginary mechanical shop.

"So you are going to give them the gold and then catch them red-handed," Chelsea cut in. "Isn't that a bit risky? I mean, they've managed to reduce your manpower by quite a bit with the hostages."

"The hostages have nothing to do with this matter," Hernandez sliced into the conversation. "That is another crime. Nothing to do with this gold matter. Just a matter of coincidence."

"I would not bet on that," Noonan noted. "These people have apparently planned well. Be that as it may, how will this ACTION FOR AMERICA get the gold and how are you going to get it back?"

"They are not going to get the gold in the first place," Hernandez snapped. He looked at Lizzard as if for confirmation and Lizzard nodded. "What is going to happen is someone from ACTION FOR AMERICA is going to look over the gold to make sure it is real, authentic. Then we are going to do the old switcheroo. We are going to replace the real gold with fake gold, lead bars painted gold. The fake gold is on an identical flatcar in the same mechanical shed," and he pointed at the imaginary mechanical shop through the terminal wall. "They will never know the real gold has been switched."

There was an extended silence and then Noonan said cautiously, "And you think they won't know they have fake gold?"

"We're working with a magician. Stage man with years of experience. He designed the bait-and-switch. Can't go wrong," Hernandez smiled like a Cheshire cat.

"Even if that's true," Chelsea cut in. "And it works . . ."

"Oh, it's going to work," Lizzard said with indignation. "It's going to work."

"I'm not doubting it will work," Chelsea continued. "But there is a legal problem. Even if you catch this ACTION WITH AMERICA with the fake gold, you are going to have a hard time in court. A good lawyer would get them off with charges of entrapment."

Lizzard did not lose the indignity in his voice. "All of the details in this operation, this matter have been discussed and handled far above your pay grade, young lady . . "

"Officer Edison," Noonan cut in. "Officer Edison is a seasoned law enforcement officer. We have no young ladies in law enforcement. Only officers."

"You are correct, Captain Noonan. Officer Edison. The details of this matter have been debated up the administrative chain of command and cleared for operation."

"I hope so," Wynter cut in. "Because 800 pounds of gold is, what, $15 million."

"Give or take," Hernandez said.

"People will kill for a lot less," Wynter continued. "And we," the index finger of his left hand swept the room with its half-dozen remaining law enforcement personnel, "are substantially understaffed."

"Not a problem," Lizzard said as he smiled. "The plan remains unchanged. They," He indicated the half-dozen officers, "will maintain a perimeter around the mechanical shed. The three of you," Lizzard indicated Noonan, Wynter and Chelsea, "will meet with the ACTION FOR AMERICA person. After he," Lizzard gave Chelsea a fleeting glance, "or she, has examined the gold, the railroad engineer hiding in the mechanical shed will switch the flatcar cable. Poof, the fake gold comes out. End of Story."

"Not all stories end with the words 'and they lived happily ever after.'" Wynter said with a sardonic grin.

"Captain Morales," Lizzard said, "you are a man with too little faith."

# CHAPTER 51

To say the least, it was the most unusual ransom note that anyone in law enforcement had ever seen. That is to say, 99% of all ransom notes fall into one of two categories. Most common were the ones which demand a certain amount of dollars for the return of a loved one. Then there begins a delicate ballet of communication with the kidnappers and family and instructions for the exchange of money for the person. The second were notes which demanded the impossible. A good example was a hostage who would be released when a certain political end was achieved. Perhaps it would be the release of a gang member from prison or a prisoner exchange between countries.

In both instances, the exchange is low-key. This is not because the press is uninterested in the kidnapping but time is so precious to all concerned that no one can wait for the end of a news cycle. Ransom exchanges, when they happen, are consummated quickly. No longer than it will take for a bank to be open to provide the cash demanded. The only time such kidnappings falter is when the family refuses to pay and goes public. This is rare and usually ineffective. It often ends with the victim being killed because he/she no longer has any value and presents a great danger to the kidnappers. Alive he/she can identify the assailants; dead he/she is the start of a homicide investigation.

As to the second type of alleged-to-be kidnapping, it is all political. These alleged-to-be kidnappings are designed for maximum publicity and are settled behind-the-scenes. Thereafter, the only mention of the alleged-to-be-kidnapping is in scholarly journals and compared to previous prisoner exchanges.

But this ransom was for pharmaceuticals. The ransom note included a long list of prescription drugs that would clearly be used to make methamphetamine. This led to the obvious conclusion that the kidnappers were druggies and had no connection whatsoever to the North Carolina Coastal Office of Homeland Security matter.

But there were five lives at risk so the threat had to be taken seriously.

# CHAPTER 52

It did not take Chloe Adrondak long to find the flaw in the room. But it was not a physical flaw as in a loose window jam or an escape hatch courtesy of a heating vent. Rather, it was in the form of a trusting aide. Adrondak was unlike the other special education clients. They really were in need of special attention. Adrondak was not. She was a con. She was in the special education program – resource actually – because it was easier to fake a condition than do algebra, conjugate verbs or read the text on the American Revolution and answer the T/F questions. Adrondak was not lazy; she was devious. She was learning it from her mother, a drama queen on her third husband. Mom was on Medicaid and Medicare, worked for cash in a Bingo parlor, sold marijuana on weekends and collected food stamps under three names. Adrondak had a progression of 'fathers,' none of whom stayed in her life long enough to give her advice. Somewhere in America she had an older brother in a jail cell and somewhere in the world she had a much older sister in the military.

For Adrondak, resource classes were an escape. She knew the rules. She had to go to school. That was a given. It was a gig, a job, a sacrifice. She had to be in the building from 8:30 to 2:30. She didn't have to do anything between 8:30 and 2:30. She just had to be there. She had a choice of where to be, regular class or special education. She chose special education because she could watch television all day long, play cards, or some number game. It was all a waste of time but that was the way the system worked. She just had to be there; she didn't have to actually do anything, learn anything. And when she got bored or was asked to do something she didn't want to do, she acted out, spit, lay on the floor on her side and kicked herself in a circle like a spinning whirligig. After all, it was resource class.

During the day, she had a shadow, an aide who followed her, stayed with her. Wherever Chloe went, the shadow went. Except on the bus. The aide never went on the bus because Chloe was on her way home and the bus driver was the supervisor. Chloe had never been a problem on the bus. Why should she be a problem on the bus? It was taking her away from the six hours of enforced boredom and manufactured hysterics. She could do what she wanted at home.

But she wasn't at home.

It wasn't as is she wanted to go home. Home was not an adventure. It was, well, just home. So she did what all prisoners do. Checked the bars on the window and lock on the door. Looked for an angle. There was always an angle. It just took time to find it. Most important, it was being prepared for the magic moment. She knew opportunity was always there; she just had to recognize it for what it was. And she had to be prepared. So she was. She wore her jacket day and night. Regardless of how warm it was inside. When she made it outside the room, it could be cold. Or raining.

She was not like the rest of the students. They were animals; she was a woman. (That's what *she* called *them*. At home. Her mother gave a grunt as a reply. To Adrondak that meant "I agree." To her mother it meant "umph" or, translated, "Don't bother me while I'm watching 'Dancing with the Stars.' Adrondak also called herself a woman even though she was 12. Her mother's response was also a grunt – which meant "umph" or, translated, "Don't bother me while I'm watching 'Dancing with the Stars.'")

The 8:30 to 2:30 'shift' at Turtle Elementary was tolerable but being cooped up with these animals after the bus ride was a bit beyond. And what was with the side trip to Greenville? The bus was going the wrong way. West instead of east. Adrondak didn't really care. At first. It was just a new way home.

Forty minutes later she did care.

And when she was shuffled into the holding facilities with the other four *animals*, she was more than concerned. She was better than this. She was only in the resource class for the shift at Turtle Elementary. That was it. Nothing more. It was a gig, what she had to do. But the gig ended with a bus ride to her neighborhood. Not to some warehouse in, where?, Greenville. Greenville! She didn't live in Greenville. She didn't know anyone in Greenville.

But the instant the door was left unguarded she was gone. She'd find someone in Greenville who'd be a friend. Or not. Maybe she'd find something entertaining. At the very least, she would not be with the four animals.

Then, just like in a poof of smoke in a magician's show, she was gone.

# CHAPTER 53

The key to success, as every successful person knows, is preparation. Successful people are not born; they are made. Self-made. They make their own luck. They do not *get* a good education, they **earn** it. It is attitude more than knowledge or hard work. There is the old saw that if you assign each letter of the alphabet with a number, A for 1, B for 2, so on and so forth, the spelling of *hard work* and *knowledge* do not equal 100%. *Attitude* does.

Highly successful people never sleep. They have a 'lean and hungry look." They are always churning possibilities over in their mind. They know the single most important rule of success is to take advantage of every situation that arrives. You do that by internalizing the single most important lesson you should learn in school.

And life.

It is called the 'elevator speech.'

And Jerome Dawson Boone had been creating elevator speeches in his mind for decades.

Imagine you are a magazine advertising salesperson. You have been trying to sell a large engineering company a full-page ad but you have not been able to make it past the front desk. You are told the muckety-muck 'has the information' and 'will get back with you when a decision is made." Which means nothing. But you are persistent because an upcoming issue would be perfect for that firm.

But you cannot get past the front desk.

On Friday evening you and your spouse/partner/girlfriend/boyfriend/buddies are enjoying yourselves when you suddenly remember you left something in your car. You excuse yourself and head downstairs. The elevator door opens and you enter. Just before the doors close, the **PRESIDENT** of that **LARGE ENGINEERING FIRM** jumps into the elevator with you. The doors close and you have **THE PRESIDENT'S** undivided attention until the elevator reaches the ground floor. That's how long you have to sell yourself, your magazine and your advertisement. You've got, at most, ten seconds. You've got to sell yourself and that ad in five – count them off on your fingers one-two-three-four-five – sentences. That's all the time you are going to have.

*Can you do it?*

If your answer is "I don't know" or "I'll have something to say when the time comes," you have already failed. Successful people – salespeople, politicians, writers, artists and assembly-line workers – constantly 'play' elevator speeches in their minds. They know there will come at a time – at least once in everyone's life – where *THE PERFECT* elevator speech is needed. They are prepared. They only need that one chance, one moment, to send their career into the ozone.

Jerome Dawson Boone was prepared. He was at the top of his game. But then again, his game had not had that many innings. But that didn't matter. He was the man of the hour. Or at least the morning. He took full advantage of the opportunity and snapped photos on his cameras, cell phone and searched for a telephoto perch in the brush outside the mechanical shed where he could get the dramatic shot of the fake flatcar being spirited out of the mechanical shed.

And he had his elevator speech ready.

The Coastal North Carolina Office of Homeland Security was going to need a public relations department and he was the only one in Coastal North Carolina with the experience needed to be a public relations department. Even if that department only had one person.

# CHAPTER 54

It did not take the North Carolina State Troopers long to gather the ransom drugs for the return of the special education children. It was simply a matter of shopping with a State of North Carolina money order. What was being demanded was legal if you had a prescription. And it was not particularly expensive – if you had a prescription. The volume was substantial but it still left the troopers wondering who they were dealing with. But then again, dealing with druggies is never logical or rational. Armed robbery of a pharmaceutical outlet for the same 'supplies' would result in an armed robbery charge which would have resulted in a sentence of about ten years, depending on the felon's record. Kidnapping was a whole different ball game. It was federal after 24 hours and carried a 30-year sentence. You were also dealing with human beings, and should one of them die in captivity, then the death penalty was on the table.

The troopers, living up to the letter of the ransom note, assembled the pharmaceuticals in question and, as per the ransom note, placed them in a rowboat at a precise location on the Tar River a dozen miles outside of Greenville. How the miscreants were going to retrieve the pharmaceuticals without being caught was anyone's guess.

As kidnapping is a crime, the troopers were in place instantly with all the equipment they needed. Including a chopper and an eye in the sky, both of which had been pulled off of the Coastal North Carolina Office of Homeland Security matter.

Whatever the matter was.

# CHAPTER 55

Jennifer and Sacerdote made good time. For good reason. It was a clear day and there was not a cloud in the sky. A perfect day for flying. She found the abandoned peanut farm with no problem and landed like the professional she was. She gunned the engine so she could roll to the far end of the field where the barn was located. When she came abreast of the barn, she did a quick turn so she was facing down the field on which she had just landed. She hit the power switch and the engine went silent. Now all she could do was sit and wait.

Sacerdote sat in the co-pilot seat silent as a child on detention. After five minutes of silence, he got a call on his cell phone. He answered the phone but all he said was "Good." He hit "end call" and punched up a new number.

The Greenville press was going to love this!

# CHAPTER 56

At 11 a.m., an hour before the ACTION FOR AMERICA contact was to meet with the commissioners of Homeland Security for Coastal North Carolina, the North Carolina State Trooper got a bead on the Rampart Transportation bus. It was located in an abandoned garage in the warehouse district of Greenville. This concentrated the power of law enforcement.

But Greenville was a city of 100,000.

This made a house-to-house search unreasonable.

So law enforcement used the best tool it had: publicity. The airwaves filled with pictures of the missing children and asking for help. There was a reward as well. Sooner or later someone would talk. It would just take some time.

# CHAPTER 57

It had only taken three days to make it from Arizona to North Carolina. He wasn't in a hurry. He took his time. Paid cash for gas and food the whole way. Slept in highway pullouts because no one asked for ID in a pullout. It was going to be the same way going home. He was as invisible as you could be in this day and age. Living off the grid helped him fade into the background.

The last night he stayed in a motel. It could not be helped. He had to be in the right position: close to the interstate, close to the railroad tracks and, once again, as invisible as you could be in this day and age. He used a fake ID to get the room. After he switched out the plates on the car. He was only going to be here for two nights and then he would be gone. All he needed was two days of anonymity. Then it would be back to Arizona. The fake ID only had to last that long. If he was stopped on his way west, his real ID would hold up and the real plates would be back on the car. He'd dump the disguise somewhere along the way. In pieces.

This was going to be an easy gig.

# CHAPTER 58

N o one from ACTION FOR AMERICA was missing.
That is, when it came to the regular, local members, they were all present. ACTION FOR AMERICA, which claimed membership in the hundreds, actually only had 18 dues-paying members.

Sort of.

Regular dues-paying members were nine and they were all there. In the Manteo State Trooper satellite station. Asking what they were doing there. Which was a good question. It was such a good question the Manteo North Carolina State Trooper satellite outpost did not have an answer. All it could say was the Commissioner for Homeland Security for Coastal North Carolina – or was it the Coastal North Carolina Commissioner for Homeland Security? – had ordered the detention. It was an office so new it did not even have stationery. But that did not stop the commissioner from relying on the State Trooper chain of command to order the detention.

Which they did.

But only for 24 hours.

And the only name not on the list of members of ACTION FOR AMERICA was a Rodolpho Sacerdote. Which was the way Rodolpho had wanted it. It had been his money that bought the computers and he was the only one who knew the passwords. Funny how the State Troopers were able to penetrate the computer so quickly, wasn't it?

# CHAPTER 59

"So this is what gold bullion looks like," Chelsea said as he nudged one of the bars with the toe of her boot. "Maybe a girl's best friend isn't a diamond."

"Only if the gold is yours," Wynter said. "I've only seen this kind of gold on television programs." He pulled back the tarp covering the gold bars and fiddled with rope tie-downs. "And this isn't bullion. Bullion is a certain purity you only get at a government mint. At least I think only the government mint can purify gold to whatever purity makes bullion."

"Well, I'd like a bar or two of these in my safety deposit box," snapped Chelsea.

"Do you even have a safety deposit box?" Noonan asked slyly.

"Nope," she replied. "But give me a few of these," she pointed at the gold bars, "and I'll get one."

# CHAPTER 60

Boone was on finger-snapping automaton. Cell phone for the troopers at a distance, cameras for the closeup. He stood slightly behind Noonan and Chelsea so they would frame the gold bars on the flatcar. Then he did a front shot, this time with the uniforms in the background. No heads, of course, because, after all, this was his story. His was going to be the face of the story. His chance at stardom. His brass ring. These photographs were his ticket to the big time or, at least, the big bucks.

Then he took a dozen selfies with the gold in the background.

And the whole time he was in the mechanical shed he said not a word to Noonan, Chelsea or Wynter. They were about to be yesterday's news. He had the photos. He had the catbird seat. He was on his way up. He had two patrons. Two! Commissioners! Not cops and some Navy guy. Yes, he was on his way out of Turtle!

# CHAPTER 61

Within a handful of moments, the surveillance power of the law enforcement had gone from countless to countable. On one hand. This was primarily due to the secrecy with which the commissioners had draped the project. No one knew exactly what the focus of the energy was so no agency had sent its 'best and brightest.' They had sent their 'political,' their people of show. The instant there was a bigger publicity nut in the tray, the people of show were gone. This left the bottom rung of staff onsite.

With the reduced personnel, they had to be used sparingly. The commissioners put four of them to cover the back of the mechanical shed. This was a daunting task because, from the back, the specific mechanical shed was simply a barn-door style entrance on a flat building which was in a bank of six identical barn doors – all closed and secure. In its heyday, the Turtle railroad mechanics were servicing multiple railways engines and cars at the same time so more than a single mechanical shed was needed. Abandoned, the 'back' of the sheds – *backs* being an inadequate term because mechanical sheds in operation had no *back* or *front*, simply multiple rail lines through the shops – were a half-dozen barn doors in sequence. There was no reason to place personnel along the *sides* of mechanical shop in question – again, the term *side* being inadequate to describe the physical setting – because the side of the mechanical shed, either of them – were at least one entire mechanical shop from where the gold on the flatcar was located.

Noonan, Wynter and Chelsea were the entire contingent monitoring the front of the mechanical shed. There was a single engineer hidden in the recess of the mechanical shop, a non-law-enforcement individual whose job consisted of two functions: stay hidden until the representative of ACTION FOR AMERICA examined the gold and then, when the representative walked out of the shop, switch the cable on the flatbed with the gold to another flatcar which had the faux gold.

In fact, Noonan, Wynter and Chelsea were not the only personnel in the foreground. Commissioners Lizzard and Hernandez were in a so-called command center, an old roundhouse, about a football field down the exit track. Boone was with them, his telephoto cameras – in the multiple with electronic 'fingers' on the shutters to capture the absconding gold from multiple angles and distances. The only other person at the front was an engineer in an ancient locomotive who had been told to be on hand to pull a flatcar toward the Greenville. He had been told nothing else. But that made no difference to him. He had been on the clock – double-time – since three a.m. – and had been instructed to 'serve at the pleasure of the Department of Homeland Security' on a 'hush-hush' project. On double-time as long as he was needed.

# CHAPTER 62

Whoever was responsible for the machinations of ACTION FOR AMERICA had planned well. Very well. The actual examination of the gold only had to be superficial. Enough of an examination to convince the watchful eye of John Law that an actual examination had occurred. That would take less than five minutes. Then the ACTION FOR AMERICA contact had to examine the flatcar cable to make sure it was attached to the flatcar with the gold. But the instant the ACTION FOR AMERICA contact turned his back on the flatcar and walked toward the locomotive ready to pull the flatcar to Greenville, the bait and switch would happen.

For the perfect getaway, three things had to happen. Rather, to *not happen*. First, there could not be fixed-wing or helicopter overhead. Particularly one with an infrared camera. With the infrared camera, the ACTION FOR AMERICA contact's approach through the Turtle forest could be monitored. Even more important, his mode of arrival, the vehicle which dropped him off, could be followed as well. But the kidnapping of the special education children had pulled all resources – including the fixed-wing and helicopter away. There was no eye in the sky.

Second, the lack of trust in the Office of Homeland Security generally and the 'hush-hush' plan in particular had placed that mission as a low priority. The kidnapping had moved it to an even lower priority. This meant the personnel left in the field were young, inexperienced and even more important, uninformed as to their mission. They were low-level functionaries who, to them, were on a meaningless errand in the middle of the night to a place in the middle of nowhere where nothing was going to happen. They would be easy to distract and the distraction only had to be for an hour which was, in the scope of things about to happen, a flash in the pan of time.

Third, the vanishing had been calculated, cunning and clever even if there was an eye in the sky.

Which there wasn't.

# CHAPTER 63

Alexander's Air Rental had no heartburn renting Jennifer Cartwright the Cessna 180, even though she would be returning the plane after hours. There was no good reason not to rent her the plane. She was a good customer, consistent and her check cleared. She had been flying for over five years, longer than some of the employees had been employees. She was known as a joyrider, the kind of person who flew for a few hours, never landed and didn't toss chicken bones or McDonald's wrappers inside the plane. She was 'grandmotherly,' Gerald Forseythe, owner of Alexander's Air Rental, told his employees. All 12 of them. "Grandmotherly. Wouldn't hurt a fly."

So, no one gave her grief when she rented the 180 and blasted into the sky over Greenville, did a 90-degree bank and headed east toward Pamlico Sound and the Atlantic Ocean.

# CHAPTER 64

Heckle and Jekyll had been in place for hours. They lived in a world of 'hurry up and wait.' That had been the railroad business. That had been the United States military. That was retirement. It was a long progression of 'hurry up and wait' moments/minutes/hours/days/months/years/decades. This morning was no different. Actually, that was not true. This was the big one, the Big Kahuna. Done right, it would be the last 'hurry up and wait' in their lives.

So they showed up on schedule, two hours before the main attraction. Sitting in the darkness dressed like Ninjas. The cables had been in place for days. The rails switched. The truck gassed and waiting. There was nothing to do but wait and watch to make sure nothing went wrong at the last moment.

And right on schedule, with an hour to go, everything went haywire. Like a scene from the Keystone Cops, the 210 feet of building-back guard of police and troopers went from a dozen to four. The rest scattered like leaves in a hurricane.

# CHAPTER 65

He came, both figurately and literally, out of the Yaupon which was, scientifically and legally, a double entendre. Yaupon's scientific name is *Ilex vomitoria*, a term that speaks for itself. He was dressed like a biker, had a ratty beard and walked with a swagger. He had a small bag at his side and did not bother to say a word to the law and order trio as he passed them on the way to the mechanical shed. Noonan followed him into the shed while Wynter and Chelsea covered Noonan's back, on the lookout for another co-conspirator who must be lurking in the woods covering the ransom checker's back. It was all very law and order predictable.

Lizzard and Hernandez were taken completely by surprise, still huddled in the command center. They did not even know the ransom checker had arrived until Boone chirped them up on the tool of Satan. Then they came running. Chelsea stopped them before they could get closer to the mechanical shed.

"Everything is in play," she said conspiratorially. "It's what you planned. Now everything is in gear. Captain Noonan is backstopping us in the shed. We don't want to crowd the pair."

"What are they doing in there?" Hernandez was exasperated. "We've got the locomotive ready to go," he pointed up the track leading to the mechanical shed. "The cable is attached. Let's get this show on the road!"

"It is going to be that easy," Wynter cautioned them. "That guy is going to check to make sure the gold on the flatcar is really gold and not lead-painted gold. He's going to take his time. Then Noonan has to distract him long enough for the cable to be switched. Noonan has to be perfect. And I do mean perfect. Everything depends on that distraction."

"That gold does not leave the shed," Lizzard said suddenly and, for the first time, nervously. "This entire, entire . . ."

". . . matter . . ." Hernandez cut it. "Matter."

"Yes, matter," Lizzard mimicked and continued. ". . .matter depends on keeping the gold from the terrorists. If the real gold comes out of the mechanical shed, this matter is over. That's final."

"Right now we don't know anything," Chelsea cut in. "The plan, your plan, is for the gold on the flatcar to remain in the shed and the lead to come out. Three seconds after a flatcar leaves the mechanical shed, we'll know if the game's afoot. Right now we wait until the bad guy OKs the gold. Then we wait and watch while Noonan works his magic . . ."

"It better be better than magic." Hernandez slammed into the conversation before Chelsea could go further. "Everything depends on that switch. That gold does not leave the shed."

Wynter gave Hernandez a side glance. "Even if it does, the gold that is, even if it does leave the shed with this guy, you can stop the flatcar anywhere along the track. That's was your backup plan wasn't it?"

It was dark but both Chelsea and Wynter could clearly see that Lizzard and Hernandez did not have a backup plan. But then, not being law and order professionals, they had no idea a back-up plan was needed. Bureaucrats never do.

# CHAPTER 66

The ransom checker said not a word when he entered the shed. His back was to Noonan so Noonan said nothing. As he entered the shed, the ransom checker reached down and picked at the cable that was required to be linked to the flatcar. It was massive and could not be lifted, not 100 feet of it. He could not lift it so he gave it a kick. Then he followed it to the flatcar. Before he started to climb onto the flatcar and turned. He didn't say anything to Noonan, just put a hand up to indicate 'stop.'

Noonan shrugged as if to say "OK" and stayed in place.

Only then did the ransom checker mount the flatcar.

# CHAPTER 67

It was not an unusual flight. Then again, if you were a pilot in California or Texas, it would have been unusual. But this was North Carolina. It was also coastal North Carolina, some communities so remote you could hear the dueling banjos in the background.

A blessing was aviation was not the way it used to be. At least not the way it was in the heyday of the Wright brothers. To them, LORAN would have been as understandable as black magic. Or, white magic, the more appropriate term. Jennifer didn't like the term 'black magic.' It was odd. First, she was black. A quadroon but in this day and age, that was black. Second, 'Magic Johnson' was black. Third, magic did not exist. It was just misguided attention. Magicians weren't, well, *magicians*. They were visual conmen. And conwomen. Things did not 'disappear' or 'reappear.' The visual plain was simply obscured, adjusted or illusionary. To the patron's eyes.

Once you became attuned to the technology of magic, razzle-dazzle disappeared. The 'magic,' not the technology. Trying to explain LORAN to the uneducated would have been difficult; GPS impossible. But everyone used GPS. It was simply black/white magic on your cell phone. How *it* knew where you were was a mystery. That it worked was undeniable.

For Jennifer, GPS, regardless of how it worked, was indispensable. She logged into the GPS destination on Google Maps and followed the verbal instructions.

While Jennifer was on a high, Sacerdote was nonplussed. To him, this was just another day in the park. Lucrative but still just a day's work. He had the enthusiasm of a ditch digger before the first shovel bit into the earth. Jennifer was lucky to be strapped into the pilot's seat. Had she not been, she would have been bouncing all over the cockpit.

To Sacerdote, it was just another operation. The only difference was that he was a step back from the action. In Vietnam and Africa and Syria, he had been in the line of fire. It had simply been a matter of progress. In Vietnam he was where the bullet clipped the underbrush. Now he was in management. Up the food chain. The man calling the shots. Those shots were just as deadly but they were not metal. Even more important, rather than hands-on, it *deus ex machina*. He set the wheels of progress in motion. He gave himself a central seat to oversee but, as far as the weeds were concerned, he was not scrounging on the ground level. Best, if things went wrong, he was a very l-o-n-g arm's length away. All the links were cauterized. So, now, it was just a movement of chess pieces on a three-dimensional board. If there was an abort, he was still in the clear. He had been here before. He was here now. He was waiting because that is all he could do as the action played out far from where he was – and that was as good as it gets.

# CHAPTER 68

Chloe Adrondak did not know where she was. But then again, she really didn't care. Not in the way a child would care if he or she became lost in the grocery store. It was not as if Chloe was dancing in the streets because of her freedom, it was more that she was not with the animals. Where was she? Who cared? She didn't? It was free time in a city.

Wherever she was – and it could not be Turtle because she had taken the school bus out of Turtle – it was not hometown either. At least not a part of her hometown she had ever seen. Again, she didn't care. There were stores here. She loved stores. She loved to shoplift. Hey, she was smarter than the cameras and faster than the security people. She knew it. Had experience doing that. And what were they going to do if they actually caught her?

Nothing.

They had nothing before.

They would do nothing now.

It was going to be Christmas in whatever neighborhood this was in whatever town this was.

Let the games begin!

# CHAPTER 69

The FBI, unlike Homeland Security, is composed of professionals. It leaves no stone unturned. Even more important than being efficient, it is timely. But not from the outside. From the outside looking in, the FBI is a cumbersome bureaucratic beast that occasionally goes public. This was not the way the FBI was supposed to work. Or law enforcement, for that matter. At least not to the man/woman in the street.

Those men and women in the street expected law and order to work like **Law and Order** on television. Or **Forensic Files.** They expected the progress of a criminal case to be like watching a poisonous snake curl and then strike. Afterall, the man/woman in the street had better things to do than wait for the cops to 'do their job.' This was a world of instant gratification, a Maypo World. Maypo was famous in the 1950s for its commercial where an adult, Uncle Ralph, takes his nephew's Mayo and likes the maple-flavored oatmeal so much he keeps it. When he cannot get his Maypo back, the nephew, Marky, loudly utters the immortal line, "I WANT MY MAYPO AND I WANT IT NOW!"

The FBI is not into theater. It works a case at the speed it works the case. It is relentless. But it is not public. And there was no reason to go public when it came to ACTION FOR AMERICA.

There was nothing to go public about.

The commissioners for Homeland Security in Manteo, Sandersonville and, lately, Turtle, had demanded it examine the computers for ACTION FOR AMERICA for illegal activity. The commissioners were no different than any other informant. Leads and documents arrive. The FBI places the lead in need of priority. The FBI examines the lead. If there is illegality, the United States Attorney is contacted. If there is no legality, sometimes a letter is sent to the informant.

In the case of the commissioners for Homeland Security in Manteo, Sandersonville, and, lately Turtle, there was nothing to report. There was not a scintilla of illegal activity on the ACTION FOR AMERICA computers. ACTION FOR AMERICA was an organization that needed watching but then again, so were a lot of other organizations. But, at this moment, there was nothing on the ACTION FOR AMERICA computers that warranted warrants, so to speak. So, from wherever the commissioners for Homeland Security in Manteo, Sandersonville, and, lately Turtle, had received the CD with the nefarious activity, that information had not come from the computers of ACTION FOR AMERICA.

So the FBI sent a letter.

When it finished the analysis.

On Friday.

It would take about five days for the letter to work its way through the proper channels.

Then the letter would be mailed and three days letter, depending on the weather, the commissioners for Homeland Security in Manteo, Sandersonville and, lately Turtle, would get the analysis.

# CHAPTER 70

Whatever he was doing the ransom checker took his time. Noonan could not see what was happening on the flatcar but he could see the tarp covering the gold bars being moved several times. After about ten minutes, the ransom checker came down off the flatcar. He approached Noonan and handed the detective a cell phone with his gloved hand. Then he waved Noonan forward.

Noonan, two steps ahead of the ransom checker stepped out of the mechanical shed and a dozen yards later, they stopped. Noonan turned to see if the ransom checker was still following but he was not. He was standing beside the track. The ransom checker angrily waved for Noonan to continue walking. Noonan did.

# CHAPTER 71

"Perfect, perfect, p-e-r-f-e-c-t," Lizzard said under his breath as Noonan and the ransom checker came out of the mechanical shed.

"Right on!" muttered Hernandez. "We just need the seconds to switch the cable. This guy is doing our job for us!"

"I hope you're right," Wynter cut in. "We're a long way from the finish line."

"In the bag, captain, in the bag," Lizzard said to Wynter. "We're in the end zone right now."

Chelsea did not say anything but Wynter could see her shaking her head. Wynter was not law enforcement but he could smell things about to go bad.

Very bad.

# CHAPTER 72

Chloe was in for a surprise. She was not in her hometown of Beaufort, a booming metropolis of 4,000 souls. She was in Greenville, a city of 100,000. Beaufort was a small town where things happened slowly. And when they did, like shoplifting children, the parents were called and pastors were responsible for the punishment. In Greenville, you called the police.

Two stores did.

The security from every store she hit followed her talking to the police on cell phones. By the time Greenville Police made it to store four, Harrison's Boutique and Hairdresser, there was a crowd on the sidewalk. What kind of an idiot was this kid and didn't she ever bother to look over her shoulder? Kids, these days, my, my, my.

# CHAPTER 73

Noonan handed the cell phone he had received from the ransom checker to Lizzard.

"He gave me this. I'm betting it's for the engineer," Noonan pointed at the locomotive two dozen yards up the track with the cell phone.

Lizzard snatched the cell phone out of Noonan's hand. "I'm in charge here," he snarled. "I'll decide who gets the cell phone."

Hernandez nodded in agreement. "Now is the time to argue about anything." He took the cell phone from Lizzard. He handed it to Chelsea. "Take this to the engineer and tell him it's probably for instructions. Then I want you back here." He looked at Noonan, Wynter and Chelsea. "We're low on people and the gold is still in the shed. We can't let anything happen to it." Then he motioned for Chelsea to get the phone to the engineer. "But you come back, hear?"

If Chelsea had a problem with being ordered around by someone not in her chain of command, she didn't show it.

Before Chelsea took a step, Noonan cut in as diplomatically as possible for him to do. "Commissioner, just a thought. If you want to catch the conspirators in the same net, you should have Officer Edison be with the gold as long as possible. I'd suggest she stay with the false gold and keep you informed as to where it is going."

It was clear Hernandez had not thought 'that far down the road.'

Uncharacteristically diplomatic, Noonan continued. "I am sure you expected the North Carolina State Troopers to handle that part of the crime. But they are gone. We," he spread his hands wide, "are all you have on this side of the mechanical shop. Someone should shadow the fake gold and keep you informed as to what is happening."

Hernandez quickly agreed. "An excellent thought." Then, to Chelsea, "Stay on the locomotive and keep me informed as to what happens."

Hernandez was not finished throwing his administrative weight around. "You, Captain, whatever your name is," He pointed at Wynter. "I need you in contact with whatever police and troopers we have left. Until that gold is picked up, the real gold, I need you to pull the door to the mechanic shed closed and I want you with your back against that door. Nobody goes into that shed without my specific instructions. Do I make myself clear?"

Wynter kind of nodded, the Navy equivalent of a 'yes, sir.' How a Navy man in a Navy uniform was supposed to coordinate with law enforcement personnel was not made clear. Hernandez didn't say; he didn't have to. He was a bureaucrat who was used to ordering underlings to do what he wanted. He never got his hands dirty; that was their job.

Hernandez continued. He stared at Noonan. "And you, Captain Noodling, I want you right here with me. Us." He corrected himself. "We need that terrorist on the flatcar with the fake gold as rapidly as possible That's your job. Hop to it."

*Captain Noodling* nodded. Now was not the time to be correcting anyone. Noonan waited until he saw Chelsea disappear into the locomotive and then come out again, giving the group a thumbs up. Noonan then turned and waved his hands at the ransom taker who was still a good dozen yards away. Noonan gave him the thumbs up. He gave Noonan two thumbs up in response and indicted with a sweep of his hands that the flatcar should get started. Noonan transferred the 'Let's go' movement to the engineer. Noonan could not see the engineer but the man, or woman, clearly got the message because in the next instant the cable linking the locomotive to the flatcar snapped tautly. The locomotive began to move slowly. As soon as it cleared the mechanic shed, the ransom checked stepped smoothly aboard. The flatcar accelerated as it passed the command group and if the ransom checker waved as he went by, none of them saw it.

# CHAPTER 74

"For this, I took a day off with no pay," Boone said to himself as he stopped snapping photos. Not that there was much for him to photograph. He had his night vision camera but, at best, he was filming people at a distance. With some of the new-fangled equipment – which cost more than a pretty penny – he might have done better. But he didn't have that equipment.

Then again, he didn't need it.

He was, so to speak, in the proverbial right place at the right time. He was locked, hip-to-hip with the biggest names in Coastal North Carolina. Who knew where that might take him? Afterall, he had the photos.

# CHAPTER 75

Chelsea could not see the ransom checker from her post in the engine cab. She was riding in an old-style locomotive, not that she knew what a new style locomotive was, but it was the kind she had seen in old movies. The engineer was old too. The kind she had seen in the movies. Black and white movies. Made in the 1940s. The engineer was the same. Just 50 years older. Same wisecracks. Happy to be working.

"I'm almost surprised the old girl is working at all," the engineer said over his shoulder. "Actually, not surprised. Made 'em good in those days. The old days. Not these days of planned obsolescence. Nope, they built things to last. Dolls, electric trains, cars. Not so today. No, no, no, too much money in buying new. Bigger, better, faster with no reason to be bigger, better or faster."

Chelsea kind of mumbled a 'yeah' or something sounding like that and kept her eyes focused on the flatcar a dozen yards behind the locomotive. How was this guy going to disappear with the gold? There was a lot of gold. You could not move that kind of gold fast. She didn't think he'd be tossing gold off the flatcar. She suspected she'd get a call and have the train stop at a remote location where a bunch of men would swarm the flatcar and pull the gold off and then disappear into the landscape. She assumed – and *assuming* is always a danger -- the cell phone was to keep in touch with the ransom taker.

# CHAPTER 76

The call came in from an anonymous source. It was probably from a cell phone, and maybe, just maybe, over a long period of time, the forces of law and order could trace the phone. But then again, if it were a throwaway, well, that would be that.

But at that moment, the concern was not tracing the call. The concern was the address given by the anonymous tip. The missing children were in an abandoned warehouse on the outskirts of Greenville.

Within 60 seconds, there was a Code Three stampede to 456 South Benson Avenue.

# CHAPTER 77

Sixty seconds, and no more, after the flatcar left the mechanical shed, the twin commissioners ordered the door of the shed closed and secured. Noonan and Wynter were ordered to stand guard as the doors were slid shut and a massive lock attached to the ancient double hinge safety hatch.

"This won't stop a fly," Wynter said after the two commissioners and Boone went back to what they called the command headquarters. "Get me a crowbar and I will be inside in moments. The lock may be new but that does not mean diddly."

"All part of the plan," Noonan told him, "Not our plan or the commissioners' plan. We are l-o-n-g way from this through with this . . .:'

". . . matter," Wynter completed Noonan's sentence.

He was right.

# CHAPTER 78

Chloe did not like cops. Never had. But then again, she had not had that many life experiences with cops. Psychiatrists, behavior experts, counselors, yes. Cops, no. But cops were different than psychiatrists, behavior experts, counselors. They didn't treat you as someone special. And she was special, you know. Everyone told her she was. Special. Special Olympics, Special Education, and special counseling. Cops did not treat people as special. They were just like everyone else.

So when Chloe got picked up for shoplifting, she was taken to the police station. Just like every other shoplifter who got caught. She had no identification so she was turned over to the Juvenile Division and she was sitting in a detention room when she heard the bus from Turtle had been found.

# CHAPTER 79

It was a perfect morning for photographs. The sun chased away the early morning darkness and started to heat the land. It was going to be a typical Coastal North Carolina day – pleasant until about 11 a.m. and then wet heat.

Boone was lounging near the commissioners, wondering what else the morning was going to bring and here he was, out of the action. He had pieced the scenario together. The gold was still in the mechanical shed and the fake gold was gone. How long it would take the bad guys to figure out they'd been hoodwinked was unknown. But that was not the point. Not for Boone. He was here, in front of the mechanical shed, and the action was up the track somewhere. All he had for his day's work was some lousy pictures which showed, quite frankly, diddly.

For this he got up early in the morning and took a day off without pay?

Then there was a mighty explosion in the back of the machine shed and in the next nanosecond, everything changed.

# CHAPTER 80

It was an explosion to wake the dead. Noonan and Wynter snapped their heads around and looked back toward the door of the mechanical shack where they had been ordered to stand. There was no damage on this side of the shed. The two were about to run around to the back of the shed when the two commissioners, quickly waddling more than running, dashed up.

"What was that?"

"No idea," Wynter said and pointed to the shed door. "Came from in there. Probably out the back."

"You two stay here. No one gets the gold, got it. No one." Lizzard was breathless.

Noonan and Wynter nodded and leaned back against the mechanical shed door.

# CHAPTER 81

Helter Skelter was the only term to describe the back of the mechanical shed. One instant there were four State Troopers and Pamlico City cops on duty watching the back bank of mechanical shed doors. Shoulder to shoulder there were six back doors, each with double tracks. Suddenly there was a loud crack, not unlike the sound of a whip tip breaking the sound barrier.

In the next instant there was an explosion.

With no warning whatsoever, one of the doors to a mechanical shed exploded outwards. Instantaneously a flatcar with a pile of gold bars erupted out of the new opening and zipped by the men on its way down the track. By the time the men had recovered from their momentary shock, all that was left of the flatcar was a canvas sheet which had been ripped by the wind of exit and was slowly settling on the ground.

# CHAPTER 82

The highways and back roads out of Greenville were chockablock with cars. But the traffic blockade was receding. Now that the special education children had been found, there was no reason to do a car-by-car search. A tip to the Greenville Police led them to the missing special education students from Turtle. The special education attendants were in shock when they were informed they were part of a kidnapping plot. When Chloe was reunited with the group, there was no one missing. Then the students were sent home in state trooper vehicles.

Thirty minutes after the flatcar exploded out of the back of the mechanical shed the roadblocks went up again. Eight hundred pounds of gold was missing. And there were 800 pounds of fake gold on its way to Greenville. There had to be a connection. No one was sure what was happening – or had happened – so there was a hold put on all traffic leaving town. Also closed were the three Greenville marinas and the airport.

# CHAPTER 83

This was Boone's moment. The instant he made it around to the back of the mechanical shed with the two commissioners he started snapping pictures. The flatcar was long gone but that didn't make any difference. At least not visually. Boone had the perfect photographic setting. He had the erupted mechanical shed door. It was expressively beautiful. Timbers had been thrust outwards and were framed like fingers pointing in the direction of the track down which the flatcar had disappeared.

He got it all on film, the exploded doorway and the commissioners on cell phones yelling orders.

"AFTER THEM!!!" Yelled the commissioners at the men standing around at the back of the mechanical shed. "THAT'S OUR GOLD!!!!"

As a unit, the men in blue peeled off, heading for their vehicles. Leaping inside they gunned down the track after the flatcar. The flatcar had a few minutes' head start but where could it go? After all it was on a railroad track.

# CHAPTER 84

Every law enforcement and Coast Guard unit got the APB at the same time. There was a flatcar of gold-headed west out of Turtle. Final destination was unknown. There were officers in pursuit but where could a flatcar go? After all, with 800 pounds of gold onboard, wherever it stopped, it would take time to offload the gold.

The eye in the sky over Greenville headed east to Turtle and the Coast Guard sent smaller craft up the Tar River to keep an eye on the railroad bridges. Best guess: the gold would be dumped from the flatcar into a river and retrieved later. If the locomotive pulling the flatcar chose its route carefully, the train would cross a trestle too narrow for state trooper vehicles. Four men could dump 800 pounds of gold in moments. Then the train could be set in motion again, this time without an engineer and the thieves could disappear into the landscape.

# CHAPTER 85

Away from the coastline and into the woods and hollers, the locomotive with the ransom checker and Chelsea slowed for an uphill
grade. Modern locomotives would have had no problem with the geographic incline, but engines built in the 1950s were victims of the terrain. Once out of flatlands the ancient behemoth had to chug rather
than run up into the foothills.

Where the ransom checker left the flatcar was not known. Best guess
was it was in the Washington area. That was the best guess because it
was not the exit that would be a problem but the escape from the area.
Getting off the flatcar was easy. As the locomotive slowed, the ransom
taker could have just rolled off the flatcar and into the brush. He was
not visible from the locomotive cab so he would not be missed. But he
was not in the clear until he could blend into the population. Leaving
the flatcar in a rural neighborhood he might have been spotted. Or his
escape vehicle stripped before he could retrieve it. No, best guess was
that he abandoned the flatcar just outside Washington. Then it would
have been an easy walk to a parking lot or motel parking lot where an
escape vehicle was parked. No one would know where he exited the
flatcar. In 24 hours it would not make any difference. He'd be halfway
to Arizona and he had his fee in cash, and cash has no enemies.

# CHAPTER 86

Jennifer was jumpy. This was not her world. Stress was not part of her life. Neither was a crime. But then again, she had been poor her whole life. Now, in a single day, she could retire with more money than she had ever dreamed of. Even more important, if the plan held together, no one would be looking for her. Or Sacerdote. They would simply live the rest of their lives on the banks of the Tar River while the combined forces of law and order spent the next decade trying to figure who had happened, what had gone wrong and who was to blame.

Sacerdote was CCC: calm, cool and collected. This was just a job. He had sent the plan in motion, now there was nothing to do but wait. He did not look at robbery as being in phases. He looked it as a finely-oiled mechanism with all the parts moving in unison. So far, all had gone according to plan.

But the game was far from over.

# CHAPTER 87

Chelsea got the bad news on the far side of Washington. She was ordered to have the locomotive pulling the faux gold bars stop and check the flatcar. She was not told why. She did as she was told. The locomotive pulling the flatcar rolled to a stop and Chelsea, gun in hand, cautiously walked the dozen yards to the flatcar.

The ransom checker was gone.

# CHAPTER 88

The last thing Noonan and Wynter were told before the two commissioners fled down the track after the itinerant flatcar was to "stay in place" in the "command center" and "wait for further instructions."

Noonan was about to say something but Wynter put a cautionary hand on Noonan's elbow. Then Noonan said something that sounded like "Yes, sir" and everyone but Noonan and Wynter vacated the Turtle machinal shed lot like sharks chasing a wounded whale.

# CHAPTER 89

Whoever had planned the escape of the gold bars had planned well. A dozen miles outside of Turtle, the train tracks made a sharp southward sweep as they went through the forest and entered an ancient trestle. The trestle was wide enough for the train but there were massive holes in the center of the track. Years of erosion had taken their toll. While the train could run on the steel rails straddling the holes, vehicles with tires could not.

So they did not.

All the State Troopers could do was look down the empty track and radio their location to the eye in the sky.

All the eye in the sky could see was forest.

All the Coast Guard could see were empty railroad bridges. But not all of them and if the river craft had been half a minute late, the train would have crossed those bridges and be gone.

# CHAPTER 90

Boone was snapping photos like a madman. Gone were the days when a photographer had to chance film capsules ever 30 or 40 frames. Today it was all electronic and Boone had his spare charger. He was capturing the event as it happened. He had the twin commissioner snapping orders and on the phone calling for backup. It was history in the making. These photos would last a lifetime – and get him a job in Sandersonville or Manteo. He'd be out of Turtle and on his way to fortune, if not fame.

# CHAPTER 91

"Ok, what are you not telling me?" Noonan did not have to worry about keeping his voice low. There were only two of them at the mechanical shed.

"Remember you told us, Chelsea and me, to be prepared for the unexpected. Well, I was." He showed Noonan his cell phone. "While we were examining the gold before the ransom man got here, I put a small GPS tracker on the flatcar."

Noonan looked at the Google Map.

"But it's not moving."

"Because," Wynter said with a smile, "because the bad boys have pulled a fast one. The flatcar that blasted out of the mechanical shed is a fraud. It's a distraction." He pointed to the cell phone. "According to this, the real gold is still inside the shed."

"Which means it's about to be stolen." Noonan smiled. "There's only one problem. We don't have a car to chase the real gold."

"But we will know where it is going. As soon as the real gold begins to move, we'll contact Chelsea to contact the Pamlico Police to close in."

"I agree. The last thing we want are the commissioners muddying up the matter."

# CHAPTER 92

It was a piece of cake. Heckle and Jekyll moved with the precision that came from years of experience. Once the back of the mechanical shed was devoid of men and women in blue, they pulled a cable out of the brush and popped open the back door to the mechanical shed. There, precisely as it had been left, was the flatcar of gold. Seconds later, the cable was attached and both men scampered back to the small locomotive. The brake was released and down the track they went. They only made two stops, both times to reset the track changing mechanism. The faux flatcar had gone west, they were going east.

# CHAPTER 93

Chelsea got the call as she was sitting on the flatcar in Washington. Her orders were to sit and wait. And that was what she was doing. And steaming. The rest of the world was chasing gold thieves and she was astride 800 pounds of lead-painted gold.

That all changed when Wynter called. She did not have to be told that the "usual channels" meant neither commissioner of Homeland Security was to be contacted.

Yet.

So she did what she had been trained to do. She passed the instructions on to the Pamlico Police to put up roadblocks around Turtle. She would have more specific details momentarily but, for the moment, no vehicle was to leave Turtle without a complete inspection. Eight hundred pounds of gold would be hard to hide.

# CHAPTER 94

Twenty minutes outside of Turtle, Heckle and Jekyll pulled the mini-locomotive to stop. Within minutes they had the eight bars, each weighing 100 pounds, off the flatcar and into a truck. They only stalled once; when they found the GPS tracker Wynter had placed.

They had expected it.

So they put it in the glove box of the truck.

Ten minutes later, they were at the landing strip. Seven bars of gold made it into the plane. Jennifer and Sacerdote waved the men goodbye. One of the men showed Sacerdote the bug and Sacerdote kind of nodded and waved his hand toward Turtle.

A minute later, Jennifer and Sacerdote were airborne, Heckle and Jekyll were bouncing down a railroad track and at the first trestle, the GPS bug went in the river below.

Heckle and Jekyll then went home and never had to worry about a roadblock because they lived in Turtle.

# CHAPTER 95

An hour later, the abandoned locomotive – with a flatcar of lead bars painted gold – was discovered abandoned on a remote stretch of track 20 miles from Turtle. It was surrounded by several hundred thousand acres of nothing but scrub brush and swamp. A second flatcar, empty, was discovered ten miles from Turtle. It was attached to a small locomotive. It was assumed that the gold had actually been on this flatcar simply because it was the only empty flatcar on a rail line leading to the mechanical shack. The gold had clearly been offloaded to a wheeled vehicle because its tracks were visible in the dust. Two sets of prints indicted two men had been responsible for the offloading.

Two hours later, the Coast Guard reported two dozen small craft had been stopped and searched on the Tar River but not a single ounce of gold was found. The Coast Guard was still checking boats on the off chance the thieves were hiding out and waiting for things to cool down.

Three hours later, the Pamlico Police announced no gold had been found in any vehicle leaving the Turtle area on any road. The police were ordered to "maintain vigilance" until ordered to stand down by the commissioners. When asked when that would be, the commissioners' response was "at the appropriate moment."

Four hours later, the North Carolina State Troopers stated it still had the Greenville, Washington, and New Bern airports sealed off and had boots on the ground at the landing strips in Williamston, Tarboro, Wilson, Snowhill, Kinston, and Bayboro. When the commissioners asked why the airports had been closed, the troopers replied that as there had been no results from the roadblocks or the Coast Guard effort, a logical conclusion was that the thieves had exited the crime area by plane. It was not possible for anyone to check every plane which had been flying in the vicinity of Turtle, so the troopers had taken the precaution of closing the larger airports for a thorough search and putting a trooper in each of the smaller airports to check outgoing flights.

Additionally, there was, at that moment, a plane-by-plane search of all aircraft at the Nags Head Wright Brothers Celebration. The troopers believed that if an aircraft was involved, it was logical that the Wright Brothers Celebration was involved because there were so many planes in the air in the area and one plane with gold could easily slip into the crowd with no one the wiser. The good news was all planes were wing-tip-to-wingtip along the landing strip and the troopers had closed the area so quickly any gold that had come in could not have been moved to motorized vehicles.

To say the commissioners were apoplectic would have been an understatement. Outwardly the term to describe them was ashen. Another term was 'walking dead.' Everyone knew the commissioners had been snookered and those who were politically astute were holding their collective breath. The higher *up* the administrative food chain a stumble was made, the more people *down* the administrative food chain would be blamed.

That blame was not long in coming.

By midafternoon Noonan and Wynter were called on the carpet for "failure to properly guard the gold they knew to be in the mechanical shed." Noonan was singled out for castigation as he had been the "face of law enforcement" at the "crime scene." Wynter was accused of insubordination for failing to inform the commissioners about the GPS bug he had planted on the flatcar with the gold.

Chelsea did not escape the wrath of the commissioners. She was accused of "dereliction of duty" for failing to tell the commissioners of the GPS bug once she knew about it and "violated protocol" by informing the Pamlico Police of the bug and having it set up roadblocks around Turtle "without the permission of the Coastal North Carolina office of Homeland Security commissioners."

The North Carolina State Troopers and Pamlico Police were put on notice they had been derelict in their duty to "honor the chain of command" when it came to "command decisions" which were to be made by "commanders" who were in the field.

Only the Manteo Police Department and the Sandersonville Police Department escaped criticism – with the exception of Noonan. As there were no other members of the Sandersonville Police Department – except Commissioner Lizzard – they and he took credit for "maintaining order in a chaotic situation." The Manteo Police Department who had no personnel on the ground – except Commissioner Hernandez – was also credited with "maintaining a cool demeanor in trying circumstances."

Boone was assigned to write up the commendations.

And produce a handful of news releases.

# CHAPTER 96

The North Carolina State Troopers would keep an eagle-eye on the rowboat of pharmaceuticals long after the special education children had been repatriated. Continuing the watch was SOP, Standard Operation Procedures. Someone had wanted those pharmaceuticals and there was the off-the-wall chance they would be tempted to retrieve the drugs. Besides, not a single felon had been apprehended in the kidnapping. Or, for that matter, in the disappearance of the 800 pounds of gold.

It was not a good day for John Law

# CHAPTER 97

Jennifer had had no trouble getting the plane aloft. Even though she had never taken off from a field before, she had ample room to get airborne even with the extra weight in the passenger compartment. There wasn't a windsock but that didn't make any difference because she could see the trees bending slightly westward so she could compensate for the drift.

Sacerdote slept most of the way to Greenville. It was only when Jennifer did a sweep to come from north that he woke up. Even then he didn't say anything. Just another day's work.

On most days the Greenville airport was a classic study of control. Takeoffs and landings were carefully orchestrated and the only business was the luggage trailers going to and from planes. Today, however, the airport was a study in chaos. The landing strip was crawling with men and women in blue who were inspecting the long line of aircraft – personal, business, commercial and industrial —which were lined up wingtip-to-wingtip on the north side of the runway.

Playing the innocent, Jennifer radioed for the reason and was told the airport was on lockdown for a "domestic terrorist incident," and she was to roll her plane to the extreme end of the runway and then park in what was usually the idle area for planes waiting their turn to take off. She asked no further questions. Sacerdote broke into a broad smile for the time all day.

# CHAPTER 98

The pro bono lawyer for ACTION FOR AMERICA had to suppress a laugh. He dropped the sheaf of paper on the table. "This is what you've got?! Are you kidding me?"

The trooper kind of rolled his eyes in the this-is-what-came-down-from-upstairs look. "This is what I've been given."

"Well," snapped the lawyer. "You've got nothing but myth and guess not a shred of evidence."

"That's not what I've been told."

"You've been told wrong! Drop the charges or go to court and look like a fool."

"I'll see what's what."

"Make it fast. I'll give you an hour. Then I file court papers." He paused before he added, "Then I'll talk to the press. ACTION FOR AMERICA does have rights."

# CHAPTER 99

B oone spent the afternoon polishing the apple. Two of them, actually, Lizzard and Hernandez. It had not taken Boone long to understand what made the commissioners tick. They wanted publicity and that could be summed up in one word: photographs. He had the photos, and he knew – and they knew – publicity was the key to success. Photos which reeked of success were far more influential than newspaper articles. Afterall, the only people who actually read the newspaper already had opinions. Pictures, however, were worth a thousand words, and in these days of news being what is on your iPhone screen, the picture was the story.

# CHAPTER 100

"Well," Chelsea said with a false sense of relief after the two commissioners had stormed out of the meeting, "I guess that tells us a thing or two."

"Carpet knights," Wynter sneered. "The same the world over."

"I'm not sure I know what that means," Noonan said. "But I can guess."

"It's an old term," Wynter replied "Real old. In the Middle Ages, most men became knights because of bravery on the battlefield. But the king's hangeroners in the royal household were made knights even though they had never been in battle. They simply knelt on the carpet in front of the King and, presto, *chango*, the King made them knight."

"Kind of like armchair generals," Chelsea cut in.

"Same concept; lots of connections and not a single hour of real-world experience."

"OK," Noonan said. "History aside, we are back to Square One when it comes to the gold. Just because they," and he tilted his head in the direction of the vanished commissioners, "have monkey-wrenched the situation, we are still on the hook."

Chelsea grimaced. "That I figured out. Unless the gold appears we are going to be the fall guys – and gal – for the next century. So, where do we start?"

"Fortunately," Noonan said with a wise smile, "we now have a crime, so we have a Square One where we can start. First, the gold has to be in one of two places: Turtle or Greenville. Turtle because the roadblocks outside of Turtle turned up nothing. Therefore, no gold came out of Turtle. But I doubt the gold is in Turtle. That leaves Greenville because that was where the school bus and the special education kids ended up. The point of the kidnapping was to pull the police off Turtle long enough for the gold to be stolen. But there was probably a second reason as well: chaos in Greenville. Every other place where the gold could be is now crawling with State Troopers."

"And those communities are small enough that the troopers and the local police can canvas the incoming and outgoing." Chelsea cut in. "I'll also bet the other towns are like Pamlico City: so small everyone knows everyone else's business."

"And here I thought you were just another pretty face," Wynter said to Chelsea. Then he added, "Logical. But let me add my two cents. Even though the GPS went into a river, I doubt the gold went into the water, fresh or salt. Whoever took the gold wanted it out of the area. They had to know the Coast Guard and troopers will be sending divers under every bridge and trestle along the rail route. It would not take that long to discover there was nothing under the water. Greenville is a good guess, but why not Nags Head? The gold had to have gotten out by plane. No other way. But there's that Wright Brothers celebration. Lots of people, lots of planes. Why not there instead of Greenville?"

"Good thought, Wynter, but you are not thinking like a criminal," Noonan told him. "Yes, to move the gold they had to use a plane. But now they have to get the gold off the plane and into some other vehicle. Yes, they could fly the gold into the celebration but the next problem is offloading the metal where everyone is watching everyone else. The troopers are checking the planes one-by-one, so I don't see the bad boys and girls taking the chance of being discovered with a routine checking. I'm betting the gold's in Greenville right now. What we have to do is get to it before it disappears."

"True," Chelsea was scratching her head. "But aren't there some loose ends here? Someone had to be involved with those locomotives. At least three people. One to move the fake flatcar and two to move the real gold. Eight hundred pounds is a bit much for one man so the real gold had to be moved by at least two men."

"The footprints were of two men," Noonan added. "I agree with you. Now we can look for the three men and they will be easy to find.

There are not that many old railroad men left in Turtle but they are not going anywhere. What we have to do is find the gold."

Wynter shook his head, "We won't have to look very far to find the mastermind, that's for sure. It's that Archie Scarborough fellow."

"I agree," Noonan said. "But he's a slippery son of an eel rancher. We've got nothing on him. He's an arm's length away from everything. Unless we catch him with gold, we've got zip."

"He's not dumb enough to get close to the robbery," Chelsea agreed. "He's the kind of a guy who makes crime pay."

"He's not out the woods yet. He expects to get something. When and how may lead us back to the gold thieves if we haven't caught them ourselves."

"Which we had better do fast." Wynter gave kind of a faux shiver. "I've been on land too long."

"Poor boy," Chelsea put an arm around his shoulder. "Time for you to charge your naval engine. Why not take a bath?"

"Not yet," Noonan gave a wry smile. "Let's get the fake gold and head to Greenville."

"You have a plan?" Wynter was surprised.

"Go to Greenville and see what's what," Noonan replied. "Just like they say in every detective novel, when you don't know what to do, go back to the beginning and see what you missed. I'm betting the caper started in Greenville, so that's where we're going."

"Why take the fake gold?" Wynter asked

"It's the only tool we have," Noonan replied.

# CHAPTER 101

Lizzard and Hernandez were in deep conversation with Boone. Boone loved it. He was at the heart of a conspiracy and these two needed him. Badly. To use a railroad expression which Boone, from Turtle, knew all too well. Things had gone 'off track.'

Lizzard and Hernandez were at a loss as to what to do. This, thought Boone to himself was very good news. For Boone. Woe-is-me people get no sympathy at all. But, at the same time, they can be easily steered.

"I have a suggestion," Boone softly spoke as the idea was already forming in his mind. It was also preliminary to orphaning an idea. He had the idea and, like a good underling, he would give the barebones to the people 'up the food chain' and let them flesh it out. That way the idea would be theirs and he, Boone, would still be in the cadre of 'special people' who are employed for their brains but never get credit for their thoughts. That was fine with Boone because Manteo or Sandersonville were more than a few steps up from his dead-end job in Turtle.

In unison, Lizzard and Hernandez turned to Boone.

"Technically," Boone said softly, "nothing has gone wrong. From the bits and pieces I have picked up from your conversation, and what is being communicated between and among the law enforcement people, the ACTION FOR AMERICA does not have the gold. Wasn't that the purpose of the entire matter? To use the gold to break up the ACTION FOR AMERICA plot to poison water and whatever else. If ACTION FOR AMERICA has no gold – and there is no reason to believe they have the gold – then the Office of Homeland Security has been success-ful. It, you, (ever the cautious appeal to the twin vanities of Lizzard and

Hernandez), have been successful. The two of you have been successful. You have achieved your goal."

Hernandez liked the idea but Lizzard was not so sure. "But the gold is missing. What do we say about that?"

Boone, if nothing else, was fast on his feet. "That's really not your concern. That's a crime, and crimes are handled by the North Carolina State Troopers and the Pamlico Police. There was only one person from the Sandersonville Police Department, the Noonan man, and he was not in Turtle as a cop. He was there as backup for the North Carolina Coastal Homeland Security group." (Boone was politically cautious. It did not do to spread the blame for failure too close to a supervisor.) "Since the theft of gold, if it was a theft, is a crime, it is not within the purview of the North Carolina Coastal Homeland Security group. It, they, you, are not a crime-fighting unit. So what happened to the gold is not your concern. So, I suggest, if anyone asks about the gold, they should be referred to the North Carolina State Troopers or Pamlico Police."

Lizzard and Hernandez now 'got the picture.' Lizzard, to use two railroad terms, went from backtracking to fast-tracking. "Absolutely. We have done our part! ACTION FOR AMERICA has been stalled in its tracks. We have averted a major catastrophe on the coast of North Carolina. We . . ."

Hernandez was quick to pick up the thought and run with it. "We should get a press release out right away. That way *we* will be helping the North Carolina State Troopers and Pamlico Police find the gold *they* are looking for."

"Boone," Lizzard sprang to action. "Can you get press releases out to the local papers . . "

". . . and some national ones?" interjected Hernandez.

Boone was not one to bypass one last opportunity for self-aggrandizement. "Why not send a selection of photographs of North Carolina Coast Homeland Security in action?" He suggested.

"An excellent idea," Lizzard said. "Don't plan on returning to Turtle too soon. We need men like you in Sandersonville."

"And Manteo," interjected Hernandez. "I see a joint public relations operation coming into existence."

He smiled.
Lizzard smiled.
Boone smiled; things were going his way.

# CHAPTER 102

Before today, Sacerdote thought, Greenville had been a somber city. Sacerdote liked that term to describe Greenville. Somber meaning dull, sober, solemn, dour, and oppressive. The kind of a city where 'nothing of importance ever happens.' Nothing ever happened in Greenville because no one was trying anything new. The population was awake at 7, on the road by 8 and in offices by 9. Then they spent until 5 shooting each other emails, letters, memos, reminders, memoranda, reports, replies, acknowledgments, thank you notes and subtle invectives. Then it was home by 6 because Greenville was not that large and bed by 9 because there was never anything interesting enough on the television to keep you awake until 11.

Sacerdote liked that. Not because it was so dull in Greenville, but because dull cities are the best ones to sow chaos. To have the police alert and stopping traffic in Raleigh, Virginia Beach or New York was par for the course. But not Greenville. Chaos brought the city to a halt and there is always profit in chaos.

It was chaos he wanted and Greenville provided. The moment the plane landed at the Greenville landing strip, it was sidetracked to the remote side of the strip. A North Carolina State Trooper was waiting for the plane at the end of the taxiway. When the engine shut down, the trooper stood on a wheel and looked into the cab.

"Sorry, ma'am," and then said "sir," when the State Trooper saw there was a man on board as well. "We're having a bit of a problem. For the moment the airport is closed. No planes in or out. I'm afraid that applies to you too," he paused for a moment, "even though you just came in. Sorry, regs."

"Not a problem," Jennifer said with a slight tremor on her upper lip. "This is just a rental."

"Sorry," the trooper stepped down off the tire. "That's the way it is for a while. Please park the plane over there," he pointed to a field where planes were being sequestered. "Leave a phone number with the officer at the desk," he pointed in the opposite direction to a small hutch, "and he'll let you know when you can return the plane."

"Not a problem," Sacerdote said from across the front of the plane. "Anything to help."

If the trooper heard what Sacerdote had said, he did not respond.

# CHAPTER 103

"We haven't been told we're off the case," Noonan said as he turned off the ringer on his cell phone – and with more than a jolt of pleasure. "So that means we are still on the clock. Just to make sure we don't get called off just yet, don't take any calls from any office of Homeland Security."

"I don't anyway," Wynter said. "Do you have a plan?"

Noonan, Wynter and Chelsea were in an unmarked on their way to Greenville. The vehicle was sluggish because of 800 pounds of lead in the trunk which caused the car to wallow a bit from side to side.

"Not a clue," Noonan returned. "But we have one hour to figure something out. I'm only confident of three things. First, the gold is not in Turtle. If it is, it's going to be found fairly quickly. The troopers are no slouches. The rock-solid lead they have are the engineers. There can't be that many people in Turtle who can run those old locomotives and know the tracks. If the gold is in Turtle, which I doubt, the troopers will find it."

"Seems logical to me," Chelsea said. "I'm betting you're going to say the gold is in Greensville."

"That's a given," Wynter said. "OK, what's the third thing you're absolutely, positively sure of?"

"We three are the best possible team to find the gold. What we have now in one hour to come up with a plan."

# CHAPTER 104

Archie Scarborough was a master of the sleight of hand. Little wonder as he had been a magician – not a particularly good one but he had made a modest living at it. Then he moved into the world of business where he quickly learned that there was magic in the real world. And sleight of hand there was called paperwork. While it was certainly true that money moved like water and everyone with a bucket was onshore, what he had learned quickly was the big money was not like water in a stream.

So you didn't stand on the shore with a bucket.

You came up with a new approach no one had thought of which, in his case, was what he had been doing in the magic industry for five decades.

It was all a matter of magic.

From the point of view of the audience.

# CHAPTER 105

Chelsea waggled her fingers after she snapped the cell phone off and looked into the back seat of the car at Wynter. "No idle worms here."

"Sorry," Wynter said in a perplexed voice. "Idle worms?"

"Idle worms. An old term. Shakespeare. You had your 'carpet knights' and I quote Shakespeare. Idle worms were worms which were supposed to grow inside of the fingers of women who were not working. I'm working so," she waggled her fingers again, "I've got no idle worms."

Noonan smiled without looking across his shoulder at Chelsea. "We're got about 15 minutes before we reach Greenville. We all know what we're supposed to do. Chelsea, thanks for being the face of law and order . . ."

Then Chelsea added, "And, in this case, unfortunately, the face of the Department of Homeland Security as well. Yes, we're good to go. I've got a State Trooper escort for Wynter and another for me. They, both of them, are going to meet us at the airport. After that, it's up to us to solve the trilemma."

"Trilemma, I like that." Noonan smiled. "But keep in mind we only have a few hours so we have to make the best of it. We are more than the face of the Office of Homeland Security. We are the only people in the Office of Homeland Security who have a ghost of a chance at retrieving the gold. And, Chelsea, no Shakespearian quotes about ghosts."

"Repent! Repent!" Chelsea said in a mimic of the ghost of McBeth.

# CHAPTER 106

I t was a *great* day.
   For Sacerdote.

A fabulous, No worries, sunshine and lollypops day. He and Jennifer were out of Turtle. He and Jennifer had the gold on the plane. The plane was not going to be searched because it was incoming. Only the outgoing planes were being searched. And as soon as the Greenville airport reopened, he and Jennifer would remove the gold and turn in the rental plane. Then they would be off. With the gold.

What could possibly go wrong?

Nothing, so he had another cup of coffee. He had the time. All he had to do was wait a few hours, and he'd be unbelievably wealthy and, even more important, in the clear.

# CHAPTER 107

Archie Scarborough put the finishing touches on his business before he took his vacation. 'Vacation' was the term he used with the office staff. Well, yes, it was going to be a vacation but not in the traditional sense of the term. He was going away and he would be back. But he would be back when the heat was down. Eight hundred pounds of gold were gone and everyone was going to look under every rock for the precious metal. Well, John Law could look under any rock in his business and home. They would find nothing because nothing was there. He'd load his car, put the bar of gold he was expecting, under the back seat and then drive south to Charleston. He wasn't going to be stopped and searched because he was nowhere near Turtle or Greenville. He was scot-free. Then, when he'd turned the gold into cash – a few ounces at a time – he'd be back in Manteo. Let 'em search. There would be nothing to find.

# CHAPTER 108

"What's the Navy doing on land?" The trooper in the assigned car was more humored than interested in Wynter in uniform. "Land pirates," Wynter retorted. "North Carolina's had a lot of them." "Still do," replied the trooper. "A lot of them are called lawyers."

"You got that one right," Wynter laughed. "Now, down to business. I want to visit these two marinas." He showed the trooper two names. "I need to visit them pronto."

"Code Three?"

"Two will do."

"Do you want anyone to know we're coming?"

"Not a chance. I want it to be a surprise."

"With Code Two?! Not a chance."

# CHAPTER 109

"Let me get this right," the Greenville police sergeant at the airport said as he looked at Noonan's badge. "You're from Sandersonville, what, 100 miles from here, not in uniform, and you say you're with the Office of Homeland Security."

"That's correct. I'm coordinating with the North Carolina State Troopers. Give them a call to get clearance. But make it quick, time is precious."

The sergeant continued the suspicious look. "If you're with Homeland Security, why am I *not* calling Homeland Security?"

Noonan smiled. "Homeland Security is a federal oversight agency. They are not law enforcement. When they need law enforcement, they call the police and Troopers. That's why you're here. If you call Homeland Security they will forward the call to the State Troopers because this matter involves Coastal North Carolina. More than one police department is involved."

"OK. I'll make the call."

# CHAPTER 110

It was Boone's finest moment.

So far.

Polish. Polish. Polish.

He did better than being singular. He wrote three press releases and attached photos. He printed off the three releases and took them into the war room at the Manteo office of the Department of Homeland Security.

Polish. Polish. Polish.

He did better. He put the releases on stationery with the heading NORTH CAROLINA COASTAL OFFICE OF HOMELAND SECURITY in bold 18 points and, below, the names of both commissioners in another typeface, bold, 16 point.

The commissioners loved the heading. And the typeface and size of the names.

They were speed-readers because it only took them seconds to read the three press releases – and they were able to see through the top sheet because they never gave the other two releases even a glance.

But they loved the photographs.

# CHAPTER 111

"We got your call from the Pamlico Police," the rental clerk said. "Pamlico. That's on the Outer Banks. What are you doing here?"

"Crime knows no boundary." Chelsea face was cop bland.

"OK. I won't ask. Yes, we have a number of pieces of equipment you could use for that job. Yes, yes, yes, I did pull the records. Six active rentals at this time. Here are copies of the agreements. Are you going to go to the other two rentals in Greenville?"

"Already been there." Cop bland again and she tapped a Manilla folder under her arm.

# CHAPTER 112

Noonan got the nod.

"You're good to go, Captain."

"Thanks. I could use your help. I need to look at any paperwork you have for the incoming flights."

"Not the outgoing? I assumed . . ."

"Well, you know what they say about the word *assume*."

"No."

"It's spelled 'a-s-s-u-m-e' and can make an *ass* of *you* and *me*."

# CHAPTER 113

Wynter was looking over the paperwork at the Tar River Marina when the call from Chelsea came in. He listened for a moment and then said, "Good work. Let me check." He pawed through the paperwork and said, in sequence, "no, no, no . . ."

Over the phone, Chelsea mimicked him. "no, no, no …."

"Zip, so far. OK, I'm off to the Greenville Marina. I'll call when I get there."

"Code Two," Chelsea added.

"Cops," said Wynter with a wry smile, "You're all the same."

# CHAPTER 14

Noonan got the call from Chelsea next.
Nothing meshed.

# CHAPTER 115

It was a great day. Good enough for a beer. But this was not a beer-drinking day. At least not yet. Sacerdote and Jennifer still had a bit of work to do. It was just a matter of time and then all would be well.

# CHAPTER 116

An hour later, Wynter and Chelsea got a hit. When Noonan got the news, he told Wynter, "Have the trooper watch the boat. You take a cab to the airport."

To Chelsea he said, "Rent the same equipment and get it to the airport."

# CHAPTER 117

When it came to the 'dark side,' a term the X Generation knows well but is a mystery to millennials – (Think STARWARS; or watch the series) – North Carolina had a distinguished history. Rather, it had a rich history of illegal enterprises. In reality, the lean to the illegal side had a lengthy and colorful history. It began – and continued – courtesy of the unique geographic features of the coastland. The British Navy, followed by the Union Navy and later the United States Coast Guard, had great difficulty stopping the widespread, ongoing illegal activities passing through Pamlico Sound and then up the rivers, streams and estuaries of Eastern North Carolina. Once ashore, the illegal goods became those which had 'fallen off a truck', and Americans – from colonists to those today – have had and did not have trouble buying goods at a discount.

Because the British had a hard time dealing with the pirates, they did not. That is, the government figured (correctly) it would be easier to make money off the illegal trade than it would be to try to suppress it. To this end, the British followed in the footsteps or, at least, the saltwater wake of the Romans. They, like the Romans, changed the vocabulary of the crime and converted it to a business. In the case of the British, the pirates were issued *Letters of Marque*, which allowed the pirates to legally steal – as long as the stealing was from other nations, not from any ship leaving the British Empire. These *Letters of Marque* transformed 'pirates' into 'privateers.' Poof! One signature on a sheet of paper and illegal actions became legal.

But there was a catch.

It was such a good idea that *Letters of Marque* are in the United States Constitution.

True to the old acronym (in English) WIFM, "What's in it for me?" the British crown demanded one-quarter of the take. If you chose to be a privateer, all was well as long as you did not steal from British Empire ships and turned over 25% of the booty to the British crown.

It did not take the privateers long to figure a way to increase their profits even if they had to pay the 25%. When the law was written, the assumption was that the privateers would be bringing their booty to England for 'conversion' to cash. This was because the bulk of the shipping at the time was in the North Atlantic and Mediterranean. This wealth of activity changed in the early 1500s when the Spanish began looting gold out of what would become Mexico and Peru. Now the attention of the privateers was laser-focused on the South Atlantic where yearly armadas of gold-laden Spanish galleons left Veracruz for Madrid.

Suddenly, there was a problem. For the privateers to remain legal they had to turn over 25% of their booty to the crown. But the crown was in England, a l-o-n-g way from the South Atlantic and every day out of the lucrative shipping lanes was one less day of plundering. So, the privateers came up with a new interpretation of the terms of the *Letters of Marque*. In reality, the privateers had never given their 25% to "the crown." That is to say; the privateers did not physically hand 25% of the gold snatched from Spanish galleons to the King himself. Or, from 1553 to 1603, to the Queens, Mary and Elizabeth. The actual transfer was made by the privateers to a minion of "the crown." There were many minions of the King and quite a few of them were a lot closer to the gold shipping lanes than London. Thus, the privateers interpreted "the crown" to be 'representatives of the crown' which, in the South Atlantic, translated to men "the crown" had appointed as governors of the colonies.

This made the governors of the colonies very happy because the cash came to them, and if some part of the 25% – or all of it – did not make it London, well, that was the way it was. Everyone 'had expenses,' as the old saying went. The privateers made the colonists very happy as well. After the 25% had been paid, the rest of the plundered cargo was sold as 'rummage,' the term then and now meaning 'used goods.' Since the privateers wanted their money as soon as possible, discounting the goods moved the merchandise. Then the privateers spent wildly. Until they were out of cash and left port after another ship – as long as that ship was not British.

This practice continued unabated until about 1700 when the British began to take a different view of privateers. There was so much plundering going on it was driving insurance rates and shipping costs higher. Then the British Navy was ordered to clean up the shipping lanes. This was not an easy chore because the privateers – and pirates – sometimes the same – had enjoyed an open field since the 1500s. The transition was hard in the colonies because so many citizens had become accustomed to cheap goods. And the governors had become accustomed to the influx of the 25% into their treasuries, colonial as well as personal.

The end of the era of the pirates is usually cited as the death of Blackbeard in 1718. Interestingly, in Pamlico Sound. Both a privateer and pirate, Edward Teach, aka Blackbeard, was a fearsome figure. He stood well over six feet tall and had jet black hair and a beard that hung to his belly. When he raided a ship, he stuck lit cannon fuses in his beard which made his face appear out of a cloud of smoke. He plundered the Caribbean and paid his 25% to the governor of North Carolina in Bath. For his largess, Teach was given a royal pardon. There is little documentation on the rumor that Teach married the governor's daughter.

While the Governor of North Carolina apparently had no problem with Teach, Alexander Spotswood, Governor of Virginia did. Why is not recorded but one might suspect he was not getting a share of the 25%. In 1718, Spotswood sent British Lieutenant Robert Maynard and a contingent of soldiers to take Teach. It did not go well for Teach. The battle took place in the vicinity of Ocracoke on November 22, and when it was over Teach was dead. His head was severed and hung from the ship's bow. Legend has it – though science disputes the fact – that when Teach's body was thrown overboard, it swam around the ship three times.

The legend of Blackbeard has given the man a dark name. In fact, there is not a single reference to any captive Blackbeard killed. He commanded his vessel with the consent of his crew and when he was killed, he had a complete pardon. For his part in the affair, Maynard was never paid for the raid on Blackbeard's ship. Interestingly, one of Blackbeard's last words were curses at Maynard's men, "Damn ye, ye yellow-bellied sapsuckers!" The image was given new life two and a half centuries later when the epithet "yellow-bellied sapsucker" became the verbal trademark of Yosemite Sam in Looney Tunes. Additionally, to this day, many visitors to Ocracoke do not know that the name originated with Blackbeard. As he was waiting for the sun to rise so he could fight Maynard in the early morning light, Blackbeard was reported to have said "Oh, cock crow." Which, today, is the origin of the name of the town Ocracoke.

A century and a half later, Pamlico Sound hosted gunrunners and blockade busters running supplies into the Confederacy and cotton to England. And 200 years after the death of Blackbeard, rumrunners were using the same unique geographic features of Pamlico Sound and the Outer Banks to protect incoming liquor from the United States Coast Guard. Noonan found it historically interesting that three hundred years after Edward Teach, gold was still being plundered in the waters, streams and estuaries of Pamlico Sound.

# CHAPTER 118

At six p.m., the State Troopers allowed the Greenville airport to reopen. The news was greeted with enthusiasm by pilots and passengers. Not so much by the vast majority of residents of Greenville who were already home and unaffected by what happened at the airport. "What happens at the airport stays at the airport."

But the big news was the finding of the special education students from Turtle. In Greenville, of all places. Why Greenville? A good question and lots of man-and-woman-in-street were asked. The overwhelming response was, "Where's Turtle?"

The second story that was just breaking was the alleged-to-be-great-news from the Coastal North Carolina Office of Homeland Security and how it had stunted a string of terrorist acts in Coastal North Carolina. Since Greenville was not 'coastal,' the story did not carry much weight. It was a story for the coast and the Outer Banks. But it was interesting,

But there was not a single mention of any gold.

# CHAPTER 119

With the hydraulic lift, Sacerdote did not need Jennifer's muscle. He pulled the pickup next to the plane, close enough for the lift's arm to make it into the passenger compartment. It was easy. He had done this before. Training and planning. Training and planning. Leave nothing to chance.

When all of the bars had been removed, Jennifer cleaned the interior of the Cessna with a portable vacuum cleaner and scrubbed the seats. No reason to leave any hint of anything for anyone. Then she shot off the runway for a last flight. She bounced over the countryside for half an hour then landed at the airport. When she landed she taxied over to the rental office. As long as she got there after 7 p.m., the office would be closed. She deposited the Cessna key in the door slot. Then she drove her car to the marina.

# CHAPTER 120

S carborough had a good laugh. What a hoot. Talk of *cajones*. Here were the two men he'd just snookered on Manteo television. Live! Standing in front of a pile of gold bars. Well, they really weren't real gold bars. Fake ones. Talking about how they, this Coastal North Carolina Office of Homeland Security, had recovered gold bars from a "nefarious terrorist group" in the "vicinity." Of course, "Of course," mouthed Scarborough, "Of course you can't say anymore because there was nothing to say to start with. But," he added with a sarcastic snarl, "what a great use of lead and paint. True stagecraft."

# CHAPTER 121

Noonan, Wynter and Chelsea spent the night in Greenville and the next morning rode with an escort to Manteo. Noonan and Wynter had not shaved in two days so stubble was visible. Chelsea's hair was flat. None of them cared.

Then they split up, Wynter going back to his ship and Chelsea to Pamlico City. They agreed to meet in Sandersonville "in a few days to wrap things up."

But before he left Manteo, Noonan had one more chore.

# CHAPTER 122

Scarborough had never seen Noonan before, so the captain had to introduce himself.

"Aren't you far from Sandersonville?" Scarborough asked, "and why aren't you in uniform?"

"I just happened to be coming through Manteo and thought I'd stop in. I'm not in uniform because I'm not on duty."

"And you are here because . . ." Sacerdote let the sentence hang.

"I'm going to tell you a little story."

"Why should I care?"

"Maybe not, but I like a good story. Don't you?"

"Does this involve a crime?"

"Am I in uniform?"

"No."

"Then it's just a story. If I were in uniform, well, that would be different."

"I'm good for a laugh."

"Good. Once upon a time, there was a man and woman who wanted to steal gold. But there's a problem with gold. It is bulky. You can't put it in your pocket and run. Not in the millions. So, they had to come up with an elaborate scheme to get oh, say, $15 million in gold."

"I'm intrigued. Go on."

Noonan smiled. "They came up with an ingenious plan to arrange for the gold to be gathered by a non-law enforcement agency, the Office of Homeland Security. That bypassed the usual checks and balances in an undercover operation."

"AH!"

"But they had a big problem. It was a classic bait-and-switch but the trick needed a pro."

"A pro?"

"You know, someone who knew about bait-and-switch. Like a retired magician."

"Like me?"

"Could have been but, as I said before, there's no crime here so this is just a story."

"I'm intrigued. Go on."

"So, this retired magician did a lot of fieldwork in Turtle and came up with a triplicating flatcar scheme."

"Clever."

"I agree. But just the bait-and-switch would not be enough. There had to be chaos among the troops. So, a fillip was added."

"Fillip?"

"Fillip, an expression meaning to add something to enhance excitement, like spice in a sauce or dash of liquor to give a blast of taste. Something added that would give a momentary boost of activity."

"Really?"

"Really. That's where the special education bus came in. It was the perfect collection of hostages, ones who never knew they were being kidnapped and even if they did, could not accurately identify anyone."

"Humm,"

"What the kidnapping did was pull all of the law enforcement personnel off the gold case. This was not unexpected because the gold matter was being handled by Homeland Security which is not law and order. The police helping the Office of Homeland Security were professionals. Guard duty was secondary to kidnapping. What this meant was when the kidnapping was discovered, the gold matter was drained of professionals.

"I see."

"Yes, and that's when the bait and switch would work. There was a skeleton crew of green law enforcement personnel watching the gold and no command-level law enforcement personnel were available. Now the bait-and-switch could work."

"Interesting; why are you telling me this?"

"Wait, my story is not finished."

"I can't wait to hear the rest."

"After the bait and switch, the gold, the real gold, was spirited out of the mechanical shed by a crew of retired locomotive engineers. It headed west to a siding where it was offloaded into a pickup and then driven to a spot where it was put on an airplane."

"How do you know that?" Sacerdote was intrigued.

Noonan tapped his forehead with his right index finger, "I'm psychic."

"Could be," Sacerdote said flatly.

"Then the gold was flown to Greenville where it sat in the plane until the airport opened. It was a clever plan, I must admit. By flying the gold into a closed airport, it had the booty in the best of all possible places. The plane would not be searched because it had been incoming. Everyone was searching outgoing flights."

Sacerdote smiled. "Clever."

"Almost. See, gold is heavy, and to move it you need men, in the plural, or a lift of some kind. To rent a lift you have to use your real name for identification. The gold bugs rented the lift for a few days, and after the airport opened, they transferred the gold from the incoming plane to another pickup. Then it was off to a marina to put the gold in a watercraft."

"Interesting."

"Yes, indeed." Noonan smiled. "But, you see, if someone in law enforcement could figure out where the gold was while the airport was shuttered, that someone could have replaced the real gold with fake gold."

Sacerdote, for the first time, showed emotion. "Oh?"

"It could have happened, you know. Fake gold replacing real gold. Kind of like the fake gold being taken for the real gold outside the mechanical shop in Turtle. It could have happened."

Sacerdote was silent.

"It could have happened, you know. And if the retired magician was expecting a cut of the pie, say a gold bar, I'd be willing to bet that the bar he gets is not gold."

Sacerdote remained silent.

"So," Noonan said as he turned to go. "I thought you'd like my story. Since no gold is gone no crime has been committed so this is, as I said before, a story."

# CHAPTER 123

S eated behind the mahogany desk in his new office in Manteo, the Public Relations Officer, Jerome Dawson Boone, entertained the visiting press with his recollection of the "Morning of the Gold Bars," as the Coastal North Carolina Office of Homeland Security had dubbed the 'matter.'

"We call it a 'matter' because we, the Coastal North Carolina Office of Homeland Security, are not a law enforcement agency. We coordinate and command but we do not investigate. No gold was lost in this matter and a great plot to disrupt Coastal North Carolina was thwarted. We, the Coastal North Carolina Office of Homeland Security, cannot discuss any of the issues in the matter, but we will be releasing a comprehensive outline of the matter and photographs next week. Make sure you leave a business card so we can get you copies of the release. In this case, truth is indeed stranger than fiction, and we have the pictures to prove it."

Someone, Boone did not know who, asked about the gold.

*Perfect*, he thought. *My perfect segue.* "The gold in this matter is evidence so it is under lock and key. It was sent to Washington D. C., the head office, for storage. Since the gold was purchased by the Coastal North Carolina Office of Homeland Security there is no loss to any individual or business in Coastal North Carolina. Well, that finishes the press conference. Be sure to leave your business cards so I can keep you informed as to the ongoing efforts of the Coastal North Carolina Office of Homeland Security."

# CHAPTER 124

Wynter and Chelsea came into the Sandersonville Grille arm-in-arm.

"I've been here before," Wynter said mockingly as he picked up a menu. "What's on your menu, Heinz?"

"Not much. You two did hear the commissioners on the news?"

"Gloating of the carpet knights," Wynter said with a snarl.

"By the way," Chelsea looked at Noonan with a questioning face, "why didn't we just take the gold out of the plane and leave? Why did we replace the fake gold for the real gold. It did take some time."

"Good question, Chelsea. The best answer is we didn't know how many people were involved in the heist. If we had just taken the gold, the bad boys and girls would know instantly it was gone. They would know we were on our way back to Manteo. They could have set up a robbery on the way back. These were incredibly clever people and they certainly had a Plan B, Plan C and maybe more. They were not people to fool with."

Chelsea was still not convinced. "You said the best answer. Do you have another?"

"Sure," Noonan smiled. "I liked the thought of them drenching their shirts for fake gold. Serves 'em right."

"Just one more thing before we wrap this up. One of the gold bars was missing," Chelsea added with a questioning look. "We recovered the gold but we only found seven bars. What happened to the eighth?"

"I'm betting the retired engineers got it." Noonan said.

"But won't they have to give it back?" Chelsea asked.

"Didn't you hear the news story," Wynter asked her. "There's no gold missing."

"Yes, there is," snapped Chelsea. "I can count."

Noonan was about to say something, but Wynter cut him off. "Chelsea, you're thinking like a cop. Stop. Things get lost in transit. That's the way it is."

"But that's gold."

"No," Noonan replied. "It's evidence that was not properly recorded. Worse, no one knew who was in charge of the gold. There were too many different agencies at the crime scene. No one agency was in charge. If a law enforcement agency had been in charge of the operation, there would have been field regulations for handling evidence. No law enforcement agency was in charge, so there was, well, no one in charge."

Wynter smiled comically. "Chelsea, stop thinking like a cop. The Coastal North Carolina Office of Homeland Security has said there is no gold missing, so there is no gold missing."

"But sooner or later, someone is going to find we are one bar short."

"Never happen," Wynter said. "Things get lost all the time. No one cares. The story is over. If anyone ever asks, there were too many fingers in the pie. Every agency will blame every other agency and as long as no one gets suddenly rich, that will be that."

"So those engineers, the ones who actually stole the gold, are going to end up with the missing bar. That's the only possibility."

"Yup," said Noonan. "You ever gone fishing, Chelsea?"

"Yeah, so what?"

"Well, you know," Noonan said with a saucy smile. "Can't catch 'em all."

www.ingramcontent.com/pod-product-compliance
Lightning Source LLC
Chambersburg PA
CBHW051641260626
47170CB00004B/1269